"I'd like to take you up on the offer of dinner."

"I see," Rico said.

"If the invitation still stands, that is."

He ought to tell her it didn't. He'd intended to wipe today from his head—every single second of it—and pursuing Carla, with her connection to the brother he wanted nothing to do with, would not be conducive to a return to his former shackle-free, nihilistic life.

But he didn't like rejection. He didn't like failure. He wasn't used to either. And the fact remained, he did still want her.

"It still stands," he said, anticipation at the thought of seeing her again and everything that might entail now thrumming through him and setting his nerve endings on fire.

"Excellent."

"Why the change of heart?"

"I'll tell you when I see you."

"I can hardly wait."

"Where should I meet you?"

"La Piccola Osteria."

"Hmm. I don't think I know it," she said, and he could hear her frown in her tone. "What's the address?"

"Calle dell'Olio. Venice."

There was a stunned silence, and then a breathy *"Venice?"*

Lost Sons of Argentina

Brothers by blood, family by choice

Identical triplets Finn, Rico and Max were born in Argentina but adopted and raised apart...

Now the long-lost brothers are starting to learn the truth about their past and each other. And the discovery their family isn't limited to the people who raised them is about to collide...with the women for whom they feel all-consuming desire!

Read Finn and Georgie's story in
The Secrets She Must Tell

And discover Rico and Carla's story in
Invitation from the Venetian Billionaire

Both available now!

And look out for Max's story

Coming soon!

Lucy King

INVITATION FROM THE VENETIAN BILLIONAIRE

HARLEQUIN
PRESENTS

HARLEQUIN®
PRESENTS®

ISBN-13: 978-1-335-56881-6

Invitation from the Venetian Billionaire

Copyright © 2021 by Lucy King

Harlequin Enterprises ULC
22 Adelaide St. West, 40th Floor
Toronto, Ontario M5H 4E3, Canada
www.Harlequin.com

Printed in U.S.A.

Lucy King spent her adolescence lost in the glamorous and exciting world of Harlequin when she really ought to have been paying attention to her teachers. But as she couldn't live in a dream world forever, she eventually acquired a degree in languages and an eclectic collection of jobs. After a decade in southwest Spain, Lucy now lives with her young family in Wiltshire, England. When not writing or trying to think up new and innovative things to do with mince, she spends her time reading, failing to finish cryptic crosswords and dreaming of the golden beaches of Andalucia.

Books by Lucy King

Harlequin Presents

Passion in Paradise
A Scandal Made in London

Lost Sons of Argentina
The Secrets She Must Tell

Other books by Lucy King

The Couple Behind the Headlines
One More Sleepless Night
The Reunion Lie
One Night with Her Ex
The Best Man for the Job
The Party Starts at Midnight

Visit the Author Profile page
at Harlequin.com for more titles.

For Katie

For the brainstorming and the chats over coffees,
walks and wine

CHAPTER ONE

'SAY CHEESE!'

Somewhat inexpertly holding her brand-new godson, Carla Blake looked at the camera and concentrated on not dropping the eleven-month-old that belonged to her best friend, Georgie, and Georgie's husband, Finn. They'd only been posing for a couple of minutes, yet already her arms ached in an effort to contain the squirming child. The strain of maintaining her smile was taking its toll on her facial muscles and her head throbbed.

Not that she wasn't happy for Georgie and Finn, or indeed to be here. She couldn't be happier. She was delighted to have been asked to be Josh's godmother, and, with everything that her best friend had been through recently, Georgie deserved every one of the bright grins wreathing her face. Finn was divine—gorgeous, supportive, utterly in love with his wife—and as for their son, who was the spitting image of his father, dark of hair, blue of eye and rosy of cheek, well, he was simply adorable.

Nor was she jealous. As picture perfect as today's christening had been so far, Carla did *not* want what Georgie had. She couldn't think of anything worse than swapping the bright lights and high-octane buzz of the city for a sprawling pile in the middle of nowhere, however beautiful.

In no conceivable way would a baby fit with her career, and she certainly didn't want a husband or partner. She didn't even want a boyfriend. Casual flings? Absolutely. Anything long term? Definitely not. She didn't have the time, and her freedom and her independence were too important to her to ever compromise.

In fact, the mere thought of putting the welfare of her emotions into the hands of a man sent chills shooting up and down her spine. Besides, she wouldn't know how to actually have a romantic relationship even if she *did* want one. Not a proper, healthy, adult one, at any rate.

No, the tension gripping her body and the pounding inside her skull were purely down to stress and exhaustion. Twenty-four hours ago she'd been in Hong Kong, massaging the ego and manipulating the mind of a truculent CEO who'd spent far too long point-blank refusing to accept that the only response to the massive data protection breach the company had just experienced was an apology to every single customer and a generous goodwill gesture to those directly affected.

Once he'd eventually seen sense and the way forward had *finally* been signed off, Carla had dashed to the airport, making her flight with minutes to spare. Having landed and cleared Customs early this morning, she'd swung by her flat to shower and change and had then driven the ninety minutes it took to reach the chocolate box Oxfordshire village Finn and Georgie had recently moved to.

She'd bust a gut to get here on time but she didn't mind one little bit because she and Georgie were more than best friends. The moment they'd met on the commune where Georgie had been living, and to which Carla and her parents moved, they'd each recognised a kindred spirit in the other and from then on they'd shared everything. Together they'd navigated the challenges of adolescence and a parenting style that bordered on neglect. Through the bleakest of times they'd provided each other with badly needed support.

However, jet lag was catching up with her now and the adrenalin that had been keeping her going was flagging. Her usual party mojo had disappeared without trace. Conversation was proving an unfamiliar slog and the heat was stifling.

But it wouldn't be long before she could go

home and crash out. And once there, *then* she'd be able to worry about possible burnout and ponder the wisdom of requesting some leave. In the meantime she would simply pull herself together and carry on smiling because today was all about Georgie and her family, and nothing—least of all, *she*—was going to ruin it.

The photographer finally gave her the thumbs-up, and as he turned away to check the pictures he'd taken Carla set Josh on the grass. While he toddled off in the direction of the gazebo where lunch was being set up, she straightened and shook out her arms, and tried not to grimace when her muscles twinged.

'My godson is as wriggly as an eel,' she said to Georgie, who'd been standing a few metres away but now stepped forward.

'He took his first solo steps a week ago,' said Georgie with a fond smile while her gaze tracked her son's progress. 'Now he just wants to practise. All the time.'

Carla watched as Josh toppled like a ninepin then got up without a whimper and resumed his journey, her amusement turning to admiration. 'His determination is impressive.'

'He takes after his father.'

'How is Finn?'

Georgie's grin faded and a small frown creased

her forehead. 'Climbing the walls while trying to pretend everything's fine.'

'Still no news?'

Late last year Finn had learned he'd been adopted as a six-month-old, and had poured considerable resources into investigating his roots. Back in March he'd discovered that he'd been born in Argentina and was one of a set of triplets, but as far as Carla was aware that was all anyone knew.

Georgie sighed. 'None.'

'It must be so frustrating.'

'It is. Finn says it doesn't matter, that he's let it go because he has us now, and I think he genuinely wants to believe that, but he isn't as good at pretending as he thinks. It's eating him up.'

And because it was eating Finn up, it was eating Georgie too, Carla knew, and she hated knowing her best friend was hurting. If only she could somehow *fix* it. 'What's being done?'

'The investigation agency is still trying to track down his brothers but the trail's gone cold.'

'Is there some way I can help? Some kind of PR campaign, maybe?'

'I don't think so,' said Georgie with a shake of her head. 'But thank you. And thank you for coming today. I know what an effort it must have been.'

'There's truly nowhere I'd rather be,' said Carla, meaning it despite the stress of the last twenty-four hours. 'It couldn't be more perfect. Josh is a very lucky little boy. Besides, you know how much I love a good party.'

And this certainly was a good party, mojo or no mojo. Not a cloud blemished the great swathe of cobalt-blue sky. The honey-coloured stone of the house gleamed in the mid-June sunshine, the glass panes of the huge sash windows glinting with warm light. The vast expanse of lawn stretched out from the terrace like an emerald carpet, bordered by hedges that had been immaculately clipped, their edges and angles a sharp contrast to the softly swishing leaves of the towering trees behind. Champagne and sparkling fruit juice flowed, mopped up by exquisitely delicate canapés, and all-round chat and laughter resounded.

'I'd better go and see to lunch,' said Georgie in response to a signal from the caterer who'd emerged from beneath the gazebo. 'Will you be all right?'

'I'll be fine,' said Carla with a reassuring smile, very glad she didn't want any of this for herself, for if she had she'd have been consumed with envy. 'Go.'

As Georgie turned to leave, Carla scanned the throng, her gaze bobbing from one elegant guest to another, when it suddenly snagged on something in the distance.

A figure stood in the shadows beyond the hedge, leaning against a tree, his arms folded across his chest, his face obscured by the dappled shade. Something about the way he was standing and watching, sort of *skulking*, triggered Carla's instinct for recognising trouble. Every sense she had switched to high alert and the tiny hairs at the back of her neck shot up.

'Wait,' she said, putting a hand on Georgie's arm to stop her just as she was about to head off.

'What?'

'Is everyone who's meant to be here, here?'

'Yes.'

'Are you expecting anyone else?'

'No.'

'Then who's that?'

Georgie looked in the direction she indicated and frowned. 'I have no idea. But I swear he wasn't there a moment ago.'

'Want me to go and check it out?'

'Are you sure?'

'Of course.' Rooting out potential problems and neutralising threats was what she did for a living, and a speedy assessment of the situation deemed any risk negligible.

'Thank you,' said Georgie with a grateful smile.

'No problem.'

'Yell if you need back-up.'

'I will.'

* * *

He'd been spotted.

From his position beneath the wide-spreading branches of the tree he'd been leaning against for the last couple of minutes, Federico Rossi clocked the exact moment the blonde noticed him. One minute she'd been chatting animatedly to her friend, the next her sweeping gaze had landed on him and she'd frozen. Long glances in his direction from both women had followed, a quick exchange of words then a nod, and now she was striding towards him, her progress impressively unhindered by her sky-high heels.

Her long limbs were loose and her hips swayed as she crossed the lawn. The top half of her red sleeveless dress moulded to her shape, but from her waist to her knees the fine fabric flowed around her thighs and drew his attention to her legs. There was nothing particularly revealing about what she was wearing but her curves were spectacular and the fluid confidence with which she moved was mesmerising.

Rico wasn't here in search of female company. He'd come solely to meet one Finn Calvert and to find out if his suspicions about who he was were correct, to ascertain the facts, and absolutely nothing else. Nevertheless, it was a relief to know that he could still appreciate an attractive woman when he saw one. Three months ago, in the immediate aftermath of the accident that had fractured his back, shattered his pelvis and broken his femur, it had been doubtful that he'd walk again, let alone regain his ability to respond quite so viscerally to a woman.

However, through sheer force of will, determination and the resilience with which he'd survived the streets of mainland Venice, which had eventually become his home following the sudden death of his parents when he was ten, he'd defied all medical expectations, and viscerally was how he was responding now.

Because as she continued to approach and he continued to watch, her face came better into focus and he saw that she was more than merely attractive. She was stunning. Sunlight bounced off choppy blonde hair that surrounded a heart-shaped face. Even at this distance he could see that her eyes, fixed unwaveringly on him, were light, possibly green, and fringed with thick dark lashes.

He couldn't have looked away even if he'd wanted to. All his attention was focused on the desire that was beginning to stir and fizz in the pit of his stomach, sending darts of heat speeding along his veins, igniting the sparks of awareness and accelerating his pulse. A dose of adrenaline shot through him and his muscles tightened as if bracing themselves for the most thrilling of attacks. And, despite the fact that her mouth was currently set in a firm, uncompromising line, he was filled with the hot, hard urge to draw her back into the shadows with him, pin her up against the tree and find out what she tasted like.

Parking that unexpectedly fierce response for later analysis and getting a swift grip on his control, since now was neither the time nor the place to find out how fully he'd recovered in that department, Rico unfolded his arms and pushed his sunglasses onto the top of his head. He thrust his hands into the pockets of his jeans to cover the inevitable effect she was having on him and levered himself off the tree trunk. He stepped forwards, out of the shadows and into the sunlight, stifling a wince as the muscles of his right leg spasmed, and at that exact same moment, a couple of feet in front of him, the woman came to an abrupt halt.

Every inch of her stilled. For the longest moment she just stared at him, as if frozen in shock. Then she raked her shimmering green gaze over him from head to toe and back up again, her eyes widening, her face paling and her mouth dropping open on a soft gasp.

'Oh, dear God,' she breathed in a way that momentarily fractured his control and filled his head with scorching images of her tangled in his sheets and moaning his name despite his intention to ignore her allure.

'Not quite,' he drawled, ruthlessly obliterating the images and focusing.

'Who *are* you?'

'Federico Rossi. My friends call me Rico.' Well, they would if he had any.

'Where did you come from?'

Originally, who knew? Who cared? He didn't. 'Venice.'

'How did you get in?'

'With unexpected ease,' he said, remembering how he'd sailed through the gates and up the drive. 'Someone left the gates open.'

'For the coming and going of staff.'

'Finn should take his security more seriously.'

'I'll let him know.' She gave her head a quick shake in an apparent effort to pull herself together. 'I can't quite believe it,' she said, nevertheless still sounding slightly stunned and appealingly breathy. 'What are you doing here?'

Well, now, *there* was a question. On the most superficial of levels Rico was here to find out if what he suspected was true. On every other level, however, he had no idea, which was confusing as hell. All he knew was that ever since he'd come across that photo in the financial press he'd been perusing while laid up in hospital, drifting in and out of pain, his broken bones recently pinned and splinted, he hadn't had a moment's peace.

Initially, he'd dismissed the electrifying jolt

that had rocked through him on first seeing the face that could almost have been his staring out at him from his laptop. He'd ignored too the strange, unsettling notion that a missing piece of him had suddenly slotted into place.

Nothing was missing from his life, he'd reassured himself while willing his heart rate to slow down and his head to clear. He had everything he could ever wish for. He neither needed nor wanted to know who this man who looked so like him might be.

However, with the interminable passing of the days that turned into weeks, the sensation swelled until it was gnawing at his gut day and night, refusing to stay unacknowledged and relentlessly taunting him with the unwelcome suggestion that here might possibly be a blood relative, whether he wanted one or not.

Eventually he hadn't been able to stand it any longer. The growing pressure to do something about it had borne down on him with increasing intensity until he'd had no choice but to give in to the instinct he hadn't yet had cause to mistrust, and take action.

An internet search of Finn Calvert had turned up nothing in the way of personal details, so he'd hired an investigation agency, which, last week, had. The seismic revelation that Finn's date of birth matched his own, leading to the conclusion that they might be more than just blood relatives, they might be brothers and quite possibly twins at that, had shaken him to the core. He still hadn't fully recovered from the shock and he certainly hadn't had the head space or time to contemplate the implications.

Not that he was telling this woman any of that. He'd sound ridiculous. He didn't have a quick answer that made any sense, so instead, with a slight smile and half a step towards her, he went for one that did.

'Right now,' he murmured, out of habit letting his gaze drift over her and noticing with interest the sudden tell-tale leap of the pulse at the base of her neck and the rush of colour that hit her pale cheeks, 'I'm admiring the scenery.'

For the briefest of moments her eyes dropped to his mouth, a flash of heat sparking in their depths. He thought he caught the tiniest hitch of her breath and sensed her moving minutely in his direction, briefly dizzying him with her scent, and it hit him like a punch to the gut that instead of suppressing the nuclear reaction going on inside him he ought to be encouraging it. Because, while he didn't fully understand the strange, primitive instinct that had compelled him to come here, to this house and its owner, he well understood desire.

He'd gone without sex for the last twelve painful weeks, and he'd missed the fierce buzz of attraction, the sizzling heat of electrifying chemistry and the blessed oblivion that inevitably followed. Here was a potential opportunity to rectify that. He hadn't planned to stay overnight in the country, intending instead to return home to Venice once he was done, but he was adaptable. He'd change his plans and invite the goddess before him to dinner in London. And afterwards, if she was amenable, he'd take her back to the penthouse apartment he owned there, tumble her into bed and prove to anyone who cared to know just how well he'd recovered from the BASE jumping accident that had nearly killed him. It would be a satisfying and enjoyable way of getting through the hours, if nothing else.

The swiftness with which she appeared to be rallying, jerking back with a quick, tiny frown, was disappointing but no great obstacle. Her captivating gaze might have turned cool, her breathing steadying and the pretty blush on her cheeks receding, but he knew what he'd seen. He knew what he'd heard. And he was going to capitalise on it.

'I meant, why the tree?' she said with impressive composure, as if she hadn't even noticed the chemistry let alone responded to it, which perversely made him only more determined to get her to agree to a date.

'What?'

'Why are you out here by a tree? What was wrong with the front door?'

Ah.

He'd had his driver park the car in front of the house at the end of a line of half a dozen others. Realising there had to be a party going on, since the investigation he'd commissioned had thrown up no suggestion that Finn was particularly into fast cars, he'd decided to assess the situation first instead of barging in. He'd walked round the side of the house, skirting the tall, wide hedge, unnoticed and surprisingly unchallenged, before identifying this tree as the best spot from which to observe the man he'd come to see, and taken up a position in the shadows, a place he was very familiar with and very comfortable in. 'Gate-crashing a party's not my style.'

Her eyebrows lifted. 'But skulking is?'

'Skulking?' It wasn't a word he'd heard before.

'Lurking. Loitering. Hiding.'

'I prefer to think of it as...observing from a distance,' he said, dismissing the flicker of apprehension that came when he realised with hindsight that perhaps he *should* have hidden, because now he'd been caught there was no backing out. No leaving without anyone being the wiser. No coming back another, quieter time. Or not at all. It was too late for regrets. He'd set these events in motion. He'd see them through. And in the meantime he'd distract himself by pursuing the beautiful woman before him.

'You're here to meet Finn.'

'I am,' he said, giving her a practised smile and feeling a surge of satisfaction when her gaze once again dipped to his mouth for a second as if she just couldn't help herself.

'Your brother.'

'Quite possibly.'

'Then you'd better come with me.'

CHAPTER TWO

WHILE CARLA HAD been making her way over, buzzing with a surge of adrenaline that wiped out her weariness and put a bounce in her step, a number of options with regard to the identity and purpose of the stranger lurking in the shadows had spun through her mind.

He was a curious neighbour, maybe. A paparazzo with pound signs in his eyes. Or something a tad more sinister, perhaps. Finn was a billionaire who owed a string of hotels, restaurants and nightclubs. Some kind of personal attack wasn't out of the question. Josh was tiny and precious and the threat of a kidnapping was real.

Never in a million years would she have guessed the truth. It was almost unbelievable. But not quite, because that this individual, this Federico Rossi, was one of Finn's long-lost brothers was undeniable.

He *had* to be.

They were identical.

Well, almost identical.

They might share eye and hair colour and possess the same imposing breadth of shoulders and towering height, but Finn didn't have the scar that featured on this man's face. His nose had never been broken and no accent tinged his English. Finn too lacked the deep tan, and sharp angles and hard lines in the bone structure department. Other than all that, though, the likeness was uncanny.

So why the man falling in beside her as she turned and set off on a discreet route back to the house should have triggered such an unexpected and intense reaction inside her when all she felt for Finn was a vague sort of fondness, Carla had no idea.

Was it the lazy confidence? The deep, gravelly, insanely sexy voice? The air of danger and the accompanying notion that, despite the laid-back exterior, Federico Rossi was a man who did and took what he wanted when he wanted and to hell with the consequences?

Whatever it was, once she'd got over her shock at his obvious identity, she'd experienced a jolt of an entirely different kind. He'd smiled at her, a slow, smouldering, stomach-melting smile, and a rush of heat had stormed through her, igniting her nerve endings and setting fire to her blood. His intense navy gaze had roamed all over her, and in its wake tiny explosions had detonated beneath her skin. By the time he'd finished his leisurely yet thorough perusal of her entire body, desire had been pounding through her and for one brief, mad moment she'd wanted to press herself up against him and seal her mouth to his.

But then some tiny nugget of self-preservation, recognising what was going on as attraction of the most lethal and inadvisable kind, to be neither entertained nor underestimated, had burst into her consciousness and she'd taken a sharp step back from the brink of madness while wondering what on earth she'd been thinking.

Everything about this man, every instinct she had, urged her to proceed with utmost caution, and that was exactly what she was going to do because she got the feeling that *he* wasn't to be entertained or underestimated either.

When it came to the opposite sex she never allowed her emotions to run riot and dictate her actions. She'd done so once before, as an affection-starved teenager who thought she'd found love where she absolutely hadn't, and that was enough. If Rico Rossi could threaten the iron-clad control she kept on her feelings with just a smile, he could be beyond dangerous, and she had zero interest in prodding the beast.

She did, however, have an interest in keeping him away from Finn and Georgie's guests, who by now were presumably having lunch but couldn't fail to be curious should he march straight into the party, the spitting image of their host, only dressed in faded blue jeans and a black polo shirt instead of a suit. So she'd deposit him in the study and then go in search of Finn to impart the surprising yet excellent news that one of his brothers had turned up, and from that moment on she need have nothing to do with him directly ever again.

'So you know my name,' he said, shortening his stride to match hers, a move that put him so close she caught a trace of his scent—male, spicy, dizzyingly intoxicating—so close she could reach out and touch him should she wish to do so, which she very definitely did not. 'What's yours?'

'Carla Blake.'

'Carla,' he echoed, rolling the 'r' around his mouth in a way that sent an involuntary shiver rippling down her spine.

'That's right,' she said with a brisk nod, deciding to inhale through her mouth and keep her eyes ahead to lessen his impact on her senses while upping her pace so that they might reach their destination that little bit quicker.

'And this party?'

'A christening. Your nephew's, probably. I'm a godparent. Georgie is my best friend. She's Josh's mother and, I'd hazard a guess, your sister-in-law.'

'A family occasion,' he muttered in a way that suggested he wasn't entirely comfortable with the idea, which was no concern of hers.

'Yes.'

'It's a beautiful day for it.'

'Indeed it is.'

'It's a beautiful day for many things.'

'Such as?'

'Making new acquaintances.'

'Your brother and his family?'

'I actually meant you, *tesoro*.'

In response to the slight deepening of his voice and the hint of silky seduction that accompanied his words, Carla's stomach tightened while heat flooded her veins.

Was he flirting with her?

Feeling strangely trembly inside, she glanced over at him to find him looking back at her, the intensity of the heat she saw in his glittering gaze nearly knocking her off her heels.

'I have plenty of acquaintances,' she said, a lot more breathlessly than she'd have preferred.

'Any like me?'

Attractive enough to turn her into a puddle of insensibility and lay siege to her control? In possession of a smile that commanded her attention against her will and rendered her all hot and quivery? Thankfully, no. 'One or two.'

The expression on his face now suggested he

didn't believe her and that knowing arrogance—even if he *was* spot-on with that assumption—was enough to blast the sense back into her.

Enough was enough, she told herself sternly as she led him towards an arch in the hedge. The reaction going on inside her was ridiculous. She didn't *do* flustered. Ever. She was cool in a crisis. She was the eye of the storm. She was *not* a pulsating mass of desire, completely at the mercy of her hormones, no matter how great the provocation.

'What are you doing when the party's over?' he asked, standing aside to let her pass through the arch ahead of him.

'Going home and crashing out,' she replied, taking great care not to let any part of her body touch any part of his on her way.

Rico ducked his head and followed her through onto the stretch of gravel that led to the house. 'That doesn't sound like much fun.'

'Perhaps not.'

'I can think of far more entertaining things to be getting up to.'

As if on cue, before she could even *think* to prevent it, her head filled with images of Rico grabbing her arm right now, drawing her into the shadows, pulling her into a tight embrace and lowering his head to give her a mind-blowing kiss while she pressed eagerly against him.

'I don't doubt it,' she said tightly, grinding her teeth in frustration as the gravel crunched beneath her feet and her body temperature rocketed. 'Nevertheless, it's what I'm doing.'

'How about dinner?'

'Toast,' she said bluntly. 'I may go wild and smash an avocado to have with it.'

'I meant you having it with me.'

'I know you did.'

'Well?'

She shook her head decisively and set her sights on the door in the side wall of the house. 'I think not.'

'Another evening, then.'

'No.'

'Are you married?'

'No.'

'Boyfriend?'

'No.'

'Girlfriend?'

'Not my thing.'

'Then why not?'

She gave the door a shove to open it and marched in. 'Do I have to have a reason?'

'Don't you?' he said, sounding genuinely curious and at the same time impossibly conceited.

Well, no, of course she didn't *have* to, although obviously she *did*. Rico's invitation to dinner might be shockingly and appallingly tempting,

despite her attempts to convince herself otherwise, but she knew first-hand the risk confident,
self-assured men like him posed. How all-consuming and seductive they could be. She knew
what it was like to succumb to the power and
charm until you no longer knew what was right
and what was wrong. To lose your identity along
with your inhibitions. To be persuaded to make
unwise choices and to believe that you were
happy about making them.

She had no intention of making the same mistake twice. She was more than content with the
steady, careful, safe life she'd created for herself.
She would allow nothing to upset it. Never again
would she be rendered powerless, vulnerable and
helpless by a man. Never again would she be manipulated into willingly giving up her freedom
and her independence, things she hadn't had the
maturity then to value.

'Does anyone ever turn you down?' she asked,
having no intention of telling him any of that and
determinedly suppressing the memories of the
distant but nevertheless frightening and confusing year she'd been groomed.

'No,' he said, closing the door behind him and
easily keeping up with her as she strode through
the house. 'But that's irrelevant and I'm not into
games. You find me as attractive as I find you,
bellissima. Dinner could prove interesting.'

His compliment made her shudder, as compliments from men—so often used with the expectation of something in return—always did, but she suppressed that too and focused. Dinner could prove disastrous and it wasn't going to happen. She would never be up for the sort of fun Rico offered, no matter how tantalisingly packaged. 'Find someone else to seduce.'

'I don't want to seduce anyone else. I want to seduce you.'

'I'd have thought you'd have other things on your mind at the moment.' Like, say, a new-found brother.

'I excel at multitasking.'

This time, thank God, she *did* manage to stifle the images of exactly how he might excel at multitasking that instantly tried to muscle their way into her head. 'My answer is still, and always will be, no.'

Without missing a step, he reached into the back pocket of his jeans and pulled out his wallet. He extracted a card and handed it to her. 'Here's my number just in case you change your mind.'

'I won't,' she said, taking it to dispose of it later, since there wasn't a bin to hand.

'You wound me.'

'You'll recover.' She stopped at the study, opened the door and stood back. 'Here we are,' she said, practically drowning with relief at fi-

nally being able to escape the dangerously sen-
suous web he was spinning around her with the
intensity of his focus and the persistence of his
pursuit. 'Wait in there. I'll go and find Finn. Once
he's got over his shock, he's going to be thrilled
you've turned up. He's been looking for you for
months. Family is *everything* to him. This is
going to be life-changing. So don't you dare go
anywhere.'

As he listened to the sharp tap of Carla's heels
marching across the polished oak floorboards of
the hall, loud at first but fading with every step
she took away from him, Rico had no doubt that
he would indeed recover from her declination of
his invitation to dinner.

Whatever it was that was slashing through him
would ease soon enough. Pique, most probably,
since generally he barely had to make any effort at all when after a date. It certainly couldn't
be disappointment that he wouldn't be getting to
know the stunningly beautiful, incredibly sexy
Carla Blake better. He didn't do disappointment.
Or regret. Or any kind of emotion, for that matter. It was of no concern to him why she'd chosen
to ignore the chemistry they shared, even though
she hadn't denied that she found him as attractive
as he did her when he'd mentioned it.

Besides, she wasn't *that* intriguing. Stunning,

yes, but their conversation, while mildly entertaining, had hardly been scintillating. He knew plenty of women who would be only too happy to while away the hours with him without engaging in any kind of conversation at all.

So it wouldn't take long for the sting of her rejection to fade, or the impact of her on his senses. Or the curve of her mouth that made him ache to know what she tasted like…the magnetic pull of her heat and her scent…the prickly obstinacy that fired his blood in a way it hadn't ever burned before…

In fact, it already *was* dissipating, and now, as he stood alone in the cool quiet of the study, taking in his surroundings while in the distance he could hear the faint clink of cutlery against crockery, the pop of a cork and the hum of chatter, with the pleasant diversion of Carla gone, his earlier unease returned tenfold.

Everywhere he looked he saw photos. On the desk, on the shelves, on the walls. Of the man who could be his double bar the scar and the broken nose, sometimes wrapped around a beautiful brunette, sometimes with a small child, mostly with both. In all of them, everyone was either smiling or laughing, clearly relaxed and happy, a tightly knit trio of emotions, history and belonging, and the closer and longer he looked, the greater the roll of his stomach and the chillier the shivers that ran down his spine.

He had no concept of such things. Living on the streets as an adolescent for four years had taught him that emotions rendered a man weak and vulnerable. They led to manipulation and exploitation, not intimacy and connection. As he understood, relationships involved attachment and commitment, compromise and understanding, none of which he'd ever experienced. They were for other people, not him, which was why Carla's reference to further potential relatives, the nephew and the sister-in-law, not to mention the nature of the occasion today, a *family* occasion, had unexpectedly knocked him for six.

He and this brother of his might look similar, but it was becoming increasingly apparent that DNA was the only thing they had in common. Judging by the photographs before him they certainly didn't share a temperament. Finn's eyes lacked the hard cynicism Rico knew lurked in the depths of his own, and the fine lines fanning out from the corner of them suggested Finn knew how to laugh and mean it. His brother wasn't a loner who preferred the shadows to the limelight. He had family. Friends. A life full of laughter and joy.

They'd evidently had very different experiences of growing up, quite apart from geography. Finn's relaxed, content exterior clearly didn't hide a great, gaping void where his soul should be. He couldn't have spent his formative years fighting for survival, sleeping with one eye open and scavenging for food in order to stave off the kind of hunger that made you hallucinate. And had Finn ever found himself part of a gang as a kid, searching for somewhere to belong, somewhere where he counted, only to be forced to do things he didn't want to do and badly let down by people in whom he'd impulsively and unwisely put his trust? It didn't seem likely.

It had been a mistake to make this trip here, Rico thought darkly, a frown creasing his forehead as he shoved his hands in his pockets and stalked over to the window in an attempt to escape the photos and the inexplicable resentment and jealousy he could feel brewing at the injustice of his and Finn's very different upbringings. A mistake to allow himself to be recklessly driven by an intuition he didn't understand to such an extent that he'd rashly dismissed the advice of his doctors to stay put and had ordered his plane that he had on permanent standby at the airport in Venice to be readied instead.

He'd acted on instinct and hadn't given a moment's thought to the ramifications. But, with hindsight, he should have because Carla's parting comment that Finn had been searching for him for months and that he'd be thrilled to have found him made his scalp prickle and his stomach churn. He wasn't interested in a sentimental reunion or a prolonged catch-up on the last thirty-one years, in back-slapping hugs and the swapping of life stories. The mere thought of engaging in a *You like chess? So do I! You're a billionaire? So am I!* kind of conversation punched the air from his lungs and drained the blood from his brain.

He didn't need anyone, least of all a sibling he'd known nothing about his entire life. He never had. Family might mean everything to Finn but Rico didn't know what it meant, full stop. Not now. He'd spent most of his life alone and he was used to it that way. He was dependent on no one and had no one dependent on him. The only person he trusted was himself and should he ever be let down now he had only himself to blame.

He didn't belong here, in a beautiful home among beautiful people who led beautiful lives that didn't deserve to be sullied by his darkness. He didn't belong anywhere. He never would. So he had nothing to gain from actually meeting Finn. Carla had already confirmed the suspicion he'd come to investigate for himself. He'd done what he'd felt compelled to do. He didn't need to hang around any longer to find out more and feel the embers of resentment and jealousy flaring into a hot, fiery burn that would scorch and destroy what little good was left in him.

In fact, if he took control of events and left right now, he could be in the air in half an hour. He'd be home by dark. And once there, he could set about resuming the life he'd led before the accident and forget that today had ever happened.

'What do you mean, he's gone?'

At the table beneath the gazebo, now cleared of lunch and instead spread with everything needed for the provision of coffee and tea, Carla stared at Georgie open-mouthed, the party and the guests milling about outside all but forgotten.

'Exactly that,' Georgie replied quietly, her face filled with confusion and worry. 'Federico Rossi is nowhere to be seen. Finn's just spent twenty minutes scouring the house and the grounds. He couldn't find him anywhere.'

Noting that her hand was trembling slightly, Carla carefully put down her coffee cup. 'I put him in the study and asked him to wait,' she said, a chill of apprehension and dismay running down her spine. 'He couldn't have just *left*.'

'I think he must have done.'

'No note?'

'No nothing,' said Georgie with a shake of her head. 'Did he give *any* indication he might leg it?'

Carla racked her brains, the conversation they'd

had spinning through her head and filling her with shame, since it should have been about Finn but instead had been all about her. 'No.'

'So why did he go?'

'I have no idea.'

'I wish he'd never come here in the first place,' Georgie muttered, her expression hardening. 'To dangle a carrot of hope like that and then whip it away… Why would anyone do that? How could he be so cruel? Why wasn't he interested in getting to know Finn? Or me and Josh? What's wrong with us? I'd sort of already slotted him into our lives if that makes sense—a relative, a *real* relative, who could maybe join us for Christmas and birthdays and things—and it was going to be so great.' She gave a big sigh. 'I'm such an idiot.'

Georgie was the *last* person in this scenario who was an idiot, thought Carla, her heart beginning to thump as the truth dawned on her. *She* was the one who'd been an idiot. And not only that, but also a shockingly and appallingly self-centred one.

Under any other circumstance she'd have considered every possible consequence of leaving Rico alone in Finn's study. She'd have weighed up what she'd learned about him, however little, and assessed the risks. Doing precisely that was part of her job, a job she'd had for the best part of a decade and supposedly excelled at.

But she hadn't. She'd fled without a moment's thought because she'd been too desperate to escape his overwhelming effect on her to think straight. For the first time in years, despite her recognition of the danger he presented, she'd let her emotions get the better of her and dictate her actions, and as a result she'd ruined everything.

What if her parting comments had been the trigger? What if Rico had been spooked by her insistence about the importance of family and her claim about how pleased Finn would be to meet him? She'd noticed his discomfort at the idea of a family occasion. If she hadn't been so derailed by her need to get away from him she'd have been more considered with her words.

'I should have locked him in,' she said, the weight of guilt and self-reproach crushing her like a rock on her chest. 'I'm so sorry.'

'It's not your fault,' said Georgie darkly. 'It's *his*.'

'How's Finn?'

'Completely gutted.'

'That's understandable,' said Carla, feeling sick at the realisation of how thoughtless and self-absorbed she'd been and how badly she'd let her friends down.

'Maybe he just needs more time.'

'It's possible.'

'And what else can we do but wait and see if he

gets back in touch at some point?' said Georgie
with a helpless shrug that cut Carla to the quick.
'It's not as if he left any contact details. All we
can do is give Alex what we have and let her get
on with it.'

Yes, they could indeed do that. With a new
name to add to the mix, no doubt Alex Osborne
of Osborne Investigations, hired by Finn to track
down his biological family, would be able to un-
earth no end of information. But she'd only be
able to find the facts. Carla could probably do
better than that.

Because Georgie was wrong.

Rico had left his number.

He'd handed her his card, which she'd intended
to toss into the bin where it belonged but had put
in her bag instead.

Why, she had no idea, but that didn't matter.
All that mattered was that she had a way of con-
tacting him, which was excellent because she
wasn't having any of this. She wasn't having Finn
and, by extension, Georgie devastated by anyone.
Georgie's pain was her pain, and her best friend
meant far too much to her to let it lie. She owed
Georgie quite possibly her *life*.

Carla had been only fifteen when she'd fallen
into the clutches of a man twice her age, who'd
spotted an opportunity to prey on a naïve, vulnerable teenager and taken it. Starved of attention

and affection by her parents, desperate to have proof that her love for them was returned and not getting it, she'd willingly been swallowed up by his flattering interest and the close emotional bond he'd deliberately and maliciously created. She hadn't questioned his requests to send him increasingly explicit pictures. She hadn't noticed she was becoming more and more isolated. When he'd finally persuaded her to run away with him she'd thought herself so sophisticated, so mature, so in love. She'd been so excited and such a fool. If it hadn't been for Georgie, who hadn't given up on her even when she'd been truly horrible, who'd eventually managed to come to her rescue, things could have turned out very differently.

Carla still didn't trust compliments and emotional intimacy. She still found it hard not to instinctively question men's interest in her and her ability to judge what was healthy when it came to relationships and what wasn't, which was why she tended to steer well clear of them, opting for short, casual flings instead. But at least, thanks to her best friend, she'd regained her self-confidence and self-esteem. At least she knew that what had happened hadn't been her fault and believed it.

Her abuser's previous victim hadn't been so fortunate. After the trial that saw him locked away for five years it had been revealed that Carla wasn't the only girl he'd preyed on. His first vic-

tim had been groomed in the same way, only she
hadn't escaped. When she'd become too old for
him and he'd left her, she'd been so messed up
she'd taken an overdose and died.

Without Georgie, that could easily have been
Carla's fate, so there was *nothing* she wouldn't
do for her. They might not share any DNA, but
they were sisters in every way that counted. In
fact, they were closer than many of the pairs of
actual siblings she knew.

So, whatever her personal feelings about Rico
Rossi, Carla could help. She wanted to. And not
only that. She needed to fix the mistakes she'd
made today. Rico had invited her out for dinner
and she'd accept. She'd use the occasion to try
and change his mind about meeting his brother.
Failing that, she'd mine him for information that
she could then pass back to Finn in the hope it
might give him at least some comfort. It wasn't
a brilliant plan, but it was a start.

She could ignore the effect he had on her, she
told herself, determination setting her jaw as it
all came together in her head. Now she'd had
some breathing space she could see that she'd
overreacted earlier. He posed no threat. He was
just a man. A devastatingly attractive one, sure,
but she was immune to that. She had no interest in the hypnotic blue of his eyes and the way
they seemed to look right into her, and she'd cer-

tainly soon forget how well his body filled out his clothes and the easy confidence with which he moved.

She was no longer an innocent teenager yearning for adventure and love, wild, gullible and ripe for the picking. She was older, savvier, stronger, and well able to withstand any attempt at seduction Rico might be foolish enough to make, especially if she reinforced the control she wielded over her emotions so that it was unbreakable. She was tenacious and focused when it came to a goal and, at the end of the day, it was only dinner.

'I might have an idea,' she said to Georgie, the need to put things right for the people she cared so much about now burning like a living flame inside her. 'Leave it with me.'

CHAPTER THREE

HIS PLANE HAVING just taken off from the small private airfield that was located conveniently close to Finn's house, Rico was travelling at a speed of three hundred kilometres per hour, staring out of the window, a glass of neat whisky in his hand, his relief at having made a lucky escape soaring with every metre they climbed.

Carla had called his aborted meeting with Finn life-changing, but he didn't need his life changed, he told himself grimly, knocking back half his drink and welcoming the heat of the alcohol that hit his stomach. He was perfectly happy with it the way it was. Or at least, the way it *had* been before the accident that had not only broken his body but also, he could recognise now, short-circuited his brain.

What on earth had he been *doing* these last few weeks? Yes, he'd had time on his hands and little to occupy his brain, given that he'd spent much of it dosed up on morphine and therefore in no fit state to work the markets, but to cede all control to an intuition he didn't even understand? He had to have been nuts.

He should have got a firmer grip on the curiosity that had burgeoned inside him on coming across that photo. He should have forgotten he'd seen it in the first place. He should certainly never have allowed any of it to dominate his thoughts to such an extent that it sent him off on a course of action that he barely understood.

Well, it all stopped now. He needed to return to being the man he'd been for the last fifteen years, who lived life on the edge and to whom nothing and no one had mattered since the moment he'd escaped the gang he'd joined, his dreams destroyed and his soul stolen, and he'd realised he was better off on his own. He needed that familiarity, that certainty, that definition of who he was. He didn't like the confusion and the doubt that had been crippling him lately.

His lingering preoccupation with Carla, with whom he'd irrefutably crashed and burned, had to stop too. Despite handing her his card, he wasn't expecting to hear from her, so he had no reason whatsoever to dwell on what might have happened had she accepted his invitation. No reason to continue contemplating her stunning green eyes and lush, kissable mouth. She wasn't the first woman he'd wanted, and she certainly wouldn't be the last. She was hardly irreplaceable. In fact, when he got home he'd set about doing precisely that.

The beep of his phone cut through his turbulent thoughts, and he switched his attention from the wide expanse of cloudless azure sky to the device on the table in front of him. He didn't recognise the UK number and on any other occasion would have let it go to voicemail, but today, now, he was more than happy to be disturbed.

With any luck, it would be someone from the London-based brokerage firm he used with something business-related. Details of a unique and complex opportunity in an emerging market, perhaps. A forex swaption recommendation. An unexpected profit warning. As long as it was something that made him money and required significant focus, he wasn't fussy.

'*Pronto.*'

'Rico? Hi. It's Carla Blake. We met earlier.'

At the sound of the voice in his ear—very much *not* the head of research at the London-based brokerage firm—every inch of him tensed and his pulse gave a great kick. Her words slid through him like silk, winding round his insides and igniting the sparks of the desire he hadn't managed to fully extinguish. He could visualise her mouth and feel her hair tickling his skin. It was as if she were actually there, beside him, leaning in close and making his groin tighten and ache, and all his efforts to put her from his mind evaporated.

'How could I possibly forget?' he said, sitting back in his seat and forcing himself to get a grip on his reaction to her and relax.

'I was hoping that might be the case.'

'Why?'

'I'd like to take you up on the offer of dinner.'

The jolt of pleasure that rocked through him at that took him by surprise. 'I see,' he said, deciding to attribute it to satisfaction that she hadn't been able to resist him after all.

'If the invitation still stands, that is.'

He ought to tell her it didn't. He'd intended to wipe today from his head—every single second of it—and pursuing Carla with her connection to the brother he wanted nothing to do with would not be conducive to a return to his former shackle-free, nihilistic life.

But he didn't like rejection. He didn't like failure. He wasn't used to either. And the fact remained, he did still want her. Badly. Plus there was the intriguing volte face. Why had she changed her mind when only at lunchtime she'd been so adamant in her refusal? Had she finally decided to accept the chemistry they shared and act on it? The potential for a night of scorching, mind-blowing sex wasn't something he was going to ignore. Reclaiming the upper hand and taking back control of their interaction wouldn't hurt either.

'It still stands,' he said, anticipation at the thought of seeing her again and everything that might entail now thrumming through him and setting his nerve endings on fire.

'Excellent.'

'Why the change of heart?'

'I'll tell you when I see you.'

'I can hardly wait.'

'Where should I meet you?'

'La Piccola Osteria.'

'Hmm. I don't think I know it,' she said, and he could hear the frown in her tone. 'What's the address?'

'Calle dell'Olio. Venice.'

There was a stunned silence, and then a breathy, *'Venice?'*

'I'm on my way home.'

'Already?'

'One of the many advantages of having a private plane,' he said, shifting in his seat to ease the ache and tension in his groin that her soft gasps had generated. 'So if you want to have dinner with me, *tesoro*, you'll need to come to Venice. Tonight. After which my invitation expires. It's your call.'

* * *

On the other end of the line, Carla stood in the cool hall of Finn and Georgie's home, every cell of her body abuzz. The effect of Rico's deep, masculine tones in her ear had been unexpectedly electrifying, sending shivers rippling up and down her spine while heating her blood, but that was nothing compared to the shock that was reeling through her now.

So much for the blithe assumption of an easy acceptance of his earlier invitation, she thought, her heart hammering wildly while her head spun. This was an entirely different prospect.

Dinner in Venice?

Tonight?

It was impossible. She'd never make it. She was knackered. The last thing she needed was another dash to another airport for another flight. The whole idea of haring halfway across a continent with next to no planning to meet a man she barely knew smacked of recklessness, something she abhorred and had taken great care to avoid after what had happened to her when she was young. She'd have to be mad to even consider it, as Georgie would no doubt tell her if she knew what Rico had just proposed.

On the other hand, when would there be another opportunity to at least try and fix the mistakes she'd made? If she didn't accept his challenge, how would she be able to change his mind or keep the lines of communication open?

She couldn't wimp out now. She had to give it a shot. The situation could hardly get worse and she could catch up on sleep any time. In fact, she might even request the next week off. And yes, she loathed the idea of giving in to any man's demands, but ultimately whether or not she went to Venice would be *her* decision. Rico wasn't forcing her to do anything. No one was. She was in total control of her choices, which was crucially important to her, and that was where she'd stay. And even if she weren't, for her best friend she'd make that sacrifice.

The fluttering in her stomach and the racing of her pulse had nothing to do with nerves. Or excitement. Or anticipation. Everything going on inside her was purely down to the crushing weight of responsibility she felt. Finn was worried that Rico could vanish into the ether for good and, because it was her fault he'd left in the first place, it was up to her to prevent that whatever it took.

'What time?'

At half-past ten Italian time, thirty minutes after she and Rico had been due to meet, Carla grabbed her suitcase and stepped off the water taxi she'd caught at the airport.

She was still barely able to believe she'd actually made it, she thought dazedly, heading for the restaurant he'd named. None of this felt real. Not the racing from Oxfordshire to her flat to the airport. Not the packed two-hour flight for which she'd been on standby and which she'd caught by the skin of her teeth. Not even the buzzing energy and the anticipation and excitement that were crashing around inside her.

The energy was a relief, but she had no business feeling excited about anything, least of all seeing Rico again. Wary? Definitely. Determined to find out why he'd run and then complete her mission? Absolutely. Anything else? Out of the question. Because this wasn't a date. Or a minibreak in a romantic city she'd never visited before. This was going to be a conversation, a retrieval of information, possibly a negotiation, nothing more, which she simply could not forget.

With her suitcase stowed in the cloakroom, Carla took a deep, steadying breath and followed the waiter out onto the terrace, channelling cool, calm control and reminding herself of the goal with every step, but no amount of preparation could have braced her for the impact of seeing Rico again.

He was lounging at a table in a far, shadowy corner of the terrace, impossibly handsome and insanely sexy in the candlelight, and when his gaze collided with hers it was as if the world suddenly skidded to a halt. Her surroundings disappeared, the twinkling fairy lights winding over and around the pergola, the clink of cutlery, the chatter of the clientele and the dashing around of the waiters gone in a heartbeat. All she could hear was the thundering of her blood in her head. All she could feel was the heavy drum of desire. All she could do was weave between tables covered with red cloths and flickering candles, as if tied to the end of a rope he was slowly hauling in.

She tried to convince herself that the flipping of her stomach was down to hunger or stress or relief that he hadn't given up on her and gone home, but she had the unsettling feeling that it was entirely down to the darkly compelling man now slowly unfolding himself and getting to his feet without taking his eyes off her for even a second.

When she reached his table, he leaned forwards, dizzying her with his spicy, masculine scent, and for one ground-tilting, heart-stopping moment she thought he was going to put his hand on her arm and drop a kiss on her cheek. In a daze, she went hot, her heart gave a great crash against her ribs and her gaze automatically went to his lips. How would they feel on her skin? Hard or soft? Would they make her burn or shiver or both?

But with a quick frown and a minute clench

of his jaw he straightened at the last minute, and the searing disappointment that spun through her nearly knocked her off her feet. Her response contained none of the relief she should have felt at the fact that he hadn't kissed her, and the realisation hit her like a bucket of icy water.

God, she had to be careful here. She was miles out of her comfort zone and on his territory. It would be so easy to lose control and herself in the highly inconvenient and deeply unwanted desire she felt for him. One slip and everything she'd worked so hard to achieve could be destroyed. One slip and she'd have more than a mistake to rectify.

She *had* to focus on why she was here and keep it at the forefront of her mind at all times. She *had* to get a grip on her reaction to him and remain composed, no matter how powerful the attraction, which surely had to lessen with familiarity.

'*Buonasera,*' she said, her voice thankfully bearing no hint of the struggle going on inside her.

'You're late,' he said with a smile so easy it made her wonder if she'd imagined his discomposure a moment ago.

'The traffic was terrible.'

'The canals can get busy at this time on a Saturday night. How was your journey?'

'Tight,' she said with a thank-you to the waiter

who whipped out the chair opposite him so she could sit down. 'As you knew it would be when you told me it was Venice or nothing.'

Rico lowered himself into his own seat and sat back, the smile curving his mouth deepening. 'Yet here you are.'

'Here I am,' she agreed, hanging her bag on the back of her chair before making herself comfortable and then fixing him with an arch look. 'As are you, which is a surprise.'

'Why would you say that?'

'You don't do waiting, do you?'

He frowned for a moment, as if he had no idea to what she was referring, and then the frown disappeared and the smile returned. 'I decided to make an exception for you.'

'I'm flattered.'

'Drink?'

God, yes. 'That would be lovely.'

'What would you like?'

'Whisky, *per favore*. Could you make it a double?'

'*Certo.*'

'*Grazie.*'

With a minute lift of his head, Rico summoned the waiter while contemplating bypassing the request for two double whiskies and simply ordering the bottle.

God knew he could do with the fortification. He was still reeling from Carla's appearance at the door of his favourite restaurant. He'd been sitting at his usual table, frowning at his watch and feeling oddly on edge, when his skin had started prickling and his pulse had leapt, a crackle of electricity suddenly charging the air around him. He'd glanced up and there she'd been, standing at the edge of the terrace, scanning the diners for him.

She'd changed from the red dress she'd been wearing earlier into tight white jeans and a silky-looking pink top over which she wore a dark jacket, but the effect she'd had on him was just as intense as it had been when he'd met her beneath the tree. The bolt of desire that had punched him in the gut was equally as powerful. The whoosh of air from his lungs had been none the less acute.

Time had slowed right down as she'd walked towards him, her gaze not leaving his for even a millisecond, and he'd been so mesmerised that instinct had taken over. Out of habit he'd got to his feet and he'd been this close to kissing her cheek when a great neon light had started flashing in his head, an intense sense of self-preservation pulling him back at the last minute.

For one thing, if he touched her he might not be able to stop, and for another, it hadn't looked as if any sort of physical contact would be welcome.

Carla's expression as she'd approached him had been severe, her gaze unwaveringly cool and her mouth once again a firm, uncompromising line, which was…unexpected.

Disappointingly, she neither sounded nor looked like someone keen on exploring the searing attraction that had arced between them, but the night was young, by Italian standards, and, at the very least, the last three months had taught him patience.

Nevertheless he was going to need his wits about him if he was going to maintain control while convincing her that taking ownership of the attraction they shared and acting on it was a good idea, which was why he decided against ordering the bottle.

When their drinks arrived a few moments later, he watched Carla pick hers up, tip back half of it and sigh with appreciation.

'Long day?' he asked, noting the faint smudges of tiredness beneath her eyes and briefly thinking about all the other ways in which he'd make her sigh once she'd come round to his way of thinking.

'Long week,' she corrected. 'I was in Hong Kong until ten o'clock last night their time.'

'Work?'

'Yes. I went straight from the airport to my flat

to the christening, then did the whole journey in reverse, only ending up here instead of there.'

'And now *I'm* flattered.'

She set her glass down and arched her eyebrow. 'I wouldn't be.'

'What made you reassess my invitation?' he said, rolling his own glass between his fingers, her spiky attitude once again only intensifying his interest. 'I was under the impression that it would be a cold day in hell before you would have dinner with me.'

Her gaze dropped to his fingers for one oddly heart-stopping moment before slowly lifting back to his. 'Toast and smashed avocado lost its appeal.'

'Really?'

'No,' she said drily. 'Of course not. Your visit was brief but devastating. You departed in a hurry and left chaos in your wake. I'd like to rectify that.'

'Why?'

'Finn is upset and Georgie's my best friend. If he's upset, she's upset, and that upsets me.'

'Enough to accept an impromptu invitation to dinner in Venice?' He couldn't even begin to imagine a relationship that deep.

'Evidently so.'

'That's some loyalty,' he said, although who was he to judge when he'd done a similar thing, compelled by an intuition he didn't even understand?

'It goes both ways.'

Not always. In his experience, loyalty was a fickle, one-sided thing that could destroy and traumatise. Life, he'd come to discover, went a lot more smoothly if you expected nothing from anyone and no one expected anything from you. Not that now was the moment to be thinking about the gang he'd joined as a youth and the mistaken belief he'd found a place to belong and a bunch of people who'd turn into family.

'So you're here to change my mind about meeting Finn,' he said, ruthlessly suppressing the harrowing memories before they could force their way into his head and focusing on Carla instead.

'Yes.'

'And there was me thinking you were interested in my charm, my wit and my devastatingly good looks.'

'I'm afraid not.'

'What a waste of a journey,' he said, ignoring the tiny dent to his ego, since he had no doubt he'd be able to change her mind. He'd caught the flicker of heat in her shimmering green gaze when she'd looked at his hand a moment ago. He'd heard the barely-there hitch of her breath. Just as when they'd been talking by the tree earlier today, she wasn't as uninterested in him as she was trying to make out.

'Not at all,' she said pleasantly. 'If I can't change your mind, I will find out as much as I can about you and report back.'

'Good luck with that.'

'Oh, I won't need luck,' she said with a smile that didn't quite reach her eyes. 'I do a similar thing on a daily basis for work.'

'I'm not one of your clients.'

'You looked me up?'

He gave a brief nod. 'I did. After leaving school at eighteen you went straight into an internship at the top PR firm in London at the time. Six years with them then you moved to your current company. You specialise in corporate damage limitation and crisis management. Your clients span the globe. Your reputation is stellar.'

'You've done your research.'

'I can't be manipulated.' Not any more.

'Everyone can be manipulated,' she said with a slight lift of her chin. 'The trick is subtlety. To make them unaware of it. I'm very good at my job.'

'So I understand,' he said easily, knowing that no one would ever be good enough to prise out *his* secrets.

'But I wouldn't take you on as a client anyway,' she said with a shrug and a sip of her drink.

'Why not?'

'In my line of work transparency is key and you're too…' she thought for a moment '…shady.'

His eyebrows lifted. 'Shady?'

'You're not the only one who decided to do some research, Rico. There's virtually no information about you online and that's strange. Normally there's something—however minor—about everyone. But apart from the one article I found that briefly described you as one of Italy's most successful but least-known hedge fund managers, your digital footprint is practically non-existent.'

Yes, well, he took care to stay out of the public eye. He didn't want anyone poking around his less than salubrious background. He'd better check out that article and have it removed. 'I value my privacy.'

'What do you have to hide? I wonder.'

What *didn't* he have to hide? Nothing he'd done as an adult had broken the law, but some of the things he'd done between the ages of twelve and sixteen as a member of the gang had. Those things were intensely personal and had caused him excruciating pain, disillusionment and shame before he'd cut off all emotion by shutting himself down. He had no intention of ever unlocking *that* door, so the last thing he wanted was Carla's curiosity aroused.

'What would you like to know?' he said expansively, feigning the transparency she was apparently so keen on in an attempt to detract her from rooting around in his psyche any further. 'Ask me anything. To you, I'm an open book.'

The look she gave him was sceptical. 'I doubt that very much.'

'Try me.'

'All right,' she said with a nod. 'Why did you turn up at Finn's house today?'

Rico inwardly tensed and fought the urge to respond to the jolt of discomfort that slammed through him. Was this her idea of subtlety? It wasn't his. But, given her reputation, perhaps he should have expected a direct hit.

'To confirm a suspicion,' he replied as casually as if she'd asked him what his favourite colour was.

'Yet you didn't stick around to do so.'

'I didn't need to. You did it for me the second we met.' The image of her standing in front of him, her green eyes wide, the pulse at the base of her neck fluttering, shot into his head and predictably sent all his blood to his groin. 'I don't think I've ever seen shock quite like it.'

'You were unexpected.'

'Evidently.'

'How did you find out about him?'

'I saw a photo of him in the press,' he said, remembering the earth-shattering moment he'd wondered firstly exactly how much morphine was in his system and secondly how the hell a picture of himself had made it into the papers. 'At the launch of his hotel in Paris.'

Carla sat back and frowned, lost in thought for a moment. 'That was taken back in March.'

He gave a brief nod. 'Correct.'

'What took you so long?'

'I've been recovering from an accident.'

'What kind of accident?'

'A bad one,' he said, lifting his glass to his mouth and knocking back a third of its contents. 'A BASE jump in the Alps went wrong.'

'A BASE jump?'

'It stands for buildings, antennae, spans and earth. Four categories of fixed objects you can jump off. Spans are bridges and earth includes mountains. Mont Blanc on this occasion. I landed badly.'

'Ouch.'

'*Esattamente,*' he agreed, although 'ouch' was something of an understatement. Having crashed into a tree and plummeted to the ground, he'd lain on the rocky terrain battered and broken, the physical pain unlike anything he'd felt before.

'I haven't been fit to travel,' he added, putting the accident from his mind, since it was in the past and he'd be done with it just as soon as the aches and twinges disappeared.

'Until today.'

Not even today, in all honesty. But the Finn-lined walls of his house in the Venice lagoon had been closing in on him and he hadn't been able to stand the not knowing any longer. 'That's right.'

'So, having spent three months recovering from an accident that must have been pretty severe if it did that much damage, you travelled to Finn's house with the intention of meeting him and then you left, without actually having done so.'

'Yes.'

She tilted her head and her gaze turned probing. 'A bit strange, after going to all that effort, don't you think?'

'Not at all,' he said, feeling a flicker of unease spring to life in his gut. 'Simply a change of plan.'

'Aren't you at all curious about him?'

Yes, very, was the answer that immediately came to mind before he shoved it back in the cupboard in his head where it belonged. 'No.'

'He's a good man.'

'I don't doubt it.'

'So why aren't you interested?'

'I don't really have the time.'

'Even if that was true, you should make time for family.'

'Do you make time for yours?'

'We're not talking about mine,' she countered

swiftly, and he could practically see the barriers flying up.

'I'll take that as a no.'

'You can take it any way you like,' she said with a defensiveness that suggested he'd hit the nail on the head.

'Interesting.'

'Not in the slightest.' She leaned forward and regarded him shrewdly. 'And you know what? I don't believe you. I don't believe you'd have made such an arduous journey the minute you could just to confirm a suspicion. If that was all you wanted to do you could have called. Or even emailed.'

'I employ a driver and own a plane,' he said in a deliberate attempt to draw her attention away from her more disconcerting observations while the discomfort inside him grew. 'It wasn't that arduous.'

'What happened between me leaving you in Finn's study and you deciding to simply walk out? Was it something I said?'

It was what she'd said and the photos, the occasion and the relatives. The sudden, stomach-curdling feeling that if he stuck around his life might irrevocably change, and quite possibly for the worse. That was what had happened. But Rico didn't want to rehash the events of earlier. He didn't even want to have to think about them. And he'd had enough of this interrogation.

He'd changed his mind about Carla's suitability as a lover, he thought darkly, ignoring the stab of disappointment that struck him in the gut and focusing on the rapid beat of his pulse and fine cold sweat now coating him instead. When he'd first laid eyes on her, he hadn't given much thought to her personality. He'd been too blown away by her looks and then too focused on distracting himself to properly acknowledge the dry, clever bite to her words.

However, now there was no denying that she was far more perceptive and tenacious than he'd anticipated, and that was way more dangerous than it was intriguing. She had the potential to see too much. Demand too much. And she'd use every weapon in her no doubt considerable arsenal to get it. No matter how intensely he set about seducing her, she wouldn't let up with the questions. If he showed any sign of succumbing to a moment of weakness she'd slip beneath his guard and have him revealing every secret he held, which simply could not happen.

However much he wanted her, he'd never put himself in a position that would leave him defenceless and exposed and vulnerable to attack. He hated the thought of being manipulated and, even worse, being unaware of it. It had happened once before, when he'd been young and desperate and an easily exploitable target, and he had no intention of allowing it to happen again.

So he'd feed her and deposit her at her hotel, bidding her goodnight instead of following her up as had been his original plan, and that really would put an end to today.

'It's getting late,' he muttered as he picked up and scoured a menu that he knew off by heart. 'We should order.'

CHAPTER FOUR

Hah...

Carla sat back, not falling for the relaxed demeanour or the dazzling yet practised smiles for a moment. Rico was hiding something. She knew it. His tells were tiny and no doubt invisible to anyone whose job wasn't all about perception and seeking out the truth behind the facade, but she'd caught the odd moment of tension that gripped his big, lean frame and the occasional flare of wariness in the depths of his eyes.

She hadn't missed the way he'd brushed off his accident as if it had been nothing more than a mild inconvenience when it had to have been anything but. Or how when she'd suggested he ought to make time for family he'd neatly turned it back on her. And the fact that he'd left unanswered her question about exactly what had made him leave Finn's study had not gone unnoticed.

He was no more an open book than she was and she may not understand *why*, but she did recognise *what* he was doing. Deflection and dissembling and carefully curating responses were tactics she deployed herself. She shared nothing of significance with the few men she dated. No details of her past, no hopes and dreams for the future and certainly no emotion. With information came power. With emotion came vulnerability, and the idea of giving a man that kind of control over her made her stomach roll. Could it be that Rico was protecting himself too?

It was none of her concern. What *was* of concern was that she badly needed to know what hidden depths lay beneath the charming exterior and the dry words, and it looked as though his armour might be harder to penetrate than she'd assumed.

But that didn't mean she was going to give up. Oh, no. If she concentrated on what was at stake tonight—Finn and Georgie and their happiness—she would get what she wanted. She usually did in the end. She hadn't been lying when she'd told Rico she believed it was all about manipulation. She knew first-hand how powerful a tactic that could be and how easy it was to shape and mould people's beliefs and behaviours, and she wasn't unaware of the irony of having made a career out of it.

However, turning a negative into a positive had been a major factor in getting over what had happened to her. She didn't feel any pangs of guilt about what she did. Controlling the narrative was key, and all the weapons she had at her disposal to achieve this were entirely compatible with the openness, honesty and transparency that were so important to her.

But manipulation probably wasn't going to work here, she reflected, picking up a menu of her own as her stomach gave a rumble and just about managing to decipher it, since pasta was pasta in almost any language. Rico was too sharp, too wary. So maybe she ought to switch tactics. She'd gone for the jugular, hoping to catch him off guard, but perhaps some of that subtlety she'd espoused a moment ago would be more successful.

As soon as they'd ordered, she'd start with some innocent questions. About his English, perhaps. Where he learned it and how it had got so good. About where he'd been raised and how he'd become involved in hedge funds. Surely he'd have no objection to providing that kind of basic information.

In the event, however, she didn't get a chance to find out. Their order was taken and the food arrived with impressive efficiency, and that was pretty much it for conversation. If Rico had been lacking in expansive answers before, he turned positively tight-lipped now. Her questions met with monosyllabic responses that dwindled into mutters, and eventually she gave up in frustrated exasperation.

She'd never seen anyone so wholly focused on their food. Each bite seemed uniquely important, a moment to be relished and protected. His head-down, methodical approach to eating was intriguing. He was utterly absorbed in the process. He didn't even notice when someone who'd clearly overdone the chianti bumped into her chair.

Although, to be fair, she barely did either.

For one thing her *spaghetti alla puttanesca* was exquisite, an all-encompassing experience of sublimely balanced flavours that exploded her taste buds and made her want to groan in pleasure. For another, with conversation non-existent, she'd found herself giving in to the temptation she'd been fighting all evening and studying him instead.

Up until now she'd had to keep her wits about her and her mind off his many attractions, but now, unobserved, she could indulge her senses. Just a little and just for a moment, because he really was unbelievably gorgeous. Beneath the white cotton of the shirt he'd changed into at some point his shoulders were wide and strong enough to carry the weight of the world. When she looked at his hands, she could envisage them on her body, sliding over her hot, bare skin and making her tremble with need. Her own hands itched with the urge to ruffle his thick, dark hair and she had to tighten her grip on her fork.

She badly wanted to know how he'd got the scar that cut a pale, jagged line at his temple and how he'd acquired the bump in his nose, the imperfections which only made him sexier. His easy, practised smile, which never quite made it to his eyes, and which she suspected was designed to both fool and conceal, was nevertheless still blinding enough to do strange things to her stomach, no matter how much she tried to resist.

For several heady minutes while they ate in silence, Carla's entire world, her focus and her attention, was reduced to the magnetising, enigmatic man sitting opposite her, so it was little wonder she'd been caught by surprise when that fellow diner had knocked into her chair.

Little wonder too that she jumped and blinked when Rico's voice cut across her surprisingly lurid thoughts.

'Are you done?'

'What?' she managed, her voice strangely husky. 'Oh. Yes.'

'Would you like anything else?'

'No, thank you,' she said, mustering up a smile of her own and fighting back a blush at having been caught staring. 'That was amazing. I'm stuffed.'

'Then I'll get the bill.'

What? The bill? That was unexpected. He'd all but promised her a seduction. She'd been braced for it and equally prepared to use it as leverage. If she was being honest, she'd been looking forward to it. To the challenge, naturally. Instead, Rico was catching the eye of a waiter and calling him over with a quick scribble in the air, clearly keen to be rid of her.

'Really?' she said, unable to prevent the frown she could feel creasing her forehead.

'It's late.'

True, but still. 'So that's it?'

'What else were you expecting?'

Good question. She was exhausted. She wasn't here on a date. She should be glad that the chemistry between them had evaporated and he no longer wanted her in that way. It mattered not one jot *why* he'd changed his mind. She wasn't interested in that in the slightest. Yet she was nowhere near achieving her mission. She'd barely even started. 'You said dinner could prove interesting.'

'I was wrong.'

'I disagree.'

'Too bad.'

Okay. So that was a bit rude, but he both sounded and looked resolute and she never begged for anything these days. Adaptability and flexibility were key in her line of work and she had both in spades. She also had his number.

Her flight was scheduled for tomorrow evening, so she had all day to bombard him with phone calls until he realised that he felt the way about the Finn situation she wanted him to. Now that she'd established contact she wasn't going to give it up without a fight. Finn and Georgie deserved more than that, and coming all this way was not going to have been for nothing.

'I see,' she said, pulling herself together and aiming for breezy. 'Well, then. Thank you for dinner.'

'You're welcome,' he said, his expression dark and unfathomable. 'I'll see you to your hotel.'

So she could be subjected to further insult along the way? She didn't think so. 'There's no need.'

'I'd like to.'

'Why?'

'You're a tourist and an easy target.'

'I may not have been to Venice,' she said a tad archly, 'but I have travelled extensively, often alone. I am perfectly capable of getting myself to a hotel in a strange city.'

'Humour me. Where are you staying?'

'The first hotel that came up with any availability.'

'Which is?'

'I don't remember the name,' she had to admit, never more regretting that she didn't have the answer to hand. 'Unsurprisingly, when I was making plans this afternoon everything was a bit of a rush. The details are on my phone. There wasn't a lot to choose from. Most places seemed to be fully booked.'

'It's high season.'

'So I gathered.'

While Rico paid the waiter, who then started whisking away their empty plates, Carla twisted to unhook her bag from the back of her chair. Her lovely, expensive designer bag that contained her passport, her cards, her cash, her keys and her phone—virtually her entire life.

Her bag that was no longer there.

It wasn't under her chair, she realised, her blood running cold, her heart pounding and the food in her stomach turning to lead. It wasn't beneath the table. It wasn't anywhere.

'What's the matter?' asked Rico, who sounded as if he were six feet below the surface of a distant canal.

'My bag,' she said dazedly as her head began to buzz. 'It's gone.'

Once Rico settled on a course of action, nothing swayed him from it, and this evening was no different. He'd decided against seducing Carla and from that moment on he just wanted supper over and done with. Her effect on him was too hard to ignore and he was tired of fighting it.

With every mouthful he'd taken, the usually delicious food tasting strangely of nothing, he'd been aware of her eyes on him, burning right through the layers of clothing and searing his skin. He was so attuned to her frequency he'd even caught the tiny variations in her breathing while she'd been studying him, which was as extraordinary as it was baffling when he'd never before experienced such awareness. But at least he'd had the consolation of soon being able to escape.

Not so now.

Fate clearly had other ideas for this evening.

'What do you mean, gone?' he asked, the unease that had faded with every passing second now slamming back into him with a vengeance.

'Exactly that,' she said, her face white, the green eyes that met his wide and troubled. 'My passport, my keys, my money, my phone. Everything. Practically my whole life. Gone.'

'How?' he said sharply. 'When?'

'I don't know.' She ran her hands through her hair, a deep frown creasing her forehead. 'But someone bumped into my chair earlier, while we were eating. I thought they were drunk. It could have happened then.'

Rico inwardly tensed, stunned disbelief ricocheting through him as the impact of her words registered. Someone had knocked into her? How the hell had he not noticed that? He, who'd once lived on the streets and still slept with one eye open. Who had razor-sharp instincts and missed nothing. He shouldn't have allowed himself to be distracted by her focus on him, *dannazione*. He shouldn't have been so determined to get through the evening as quickly as possible, to the extent that nothing else mattered.

'Do you remember what they looked like?' he asked, not liking one little bit the apparent dulling of the wits he'd relied on from the age of twelve.

'Not really. I barely caught a glimpse of him. Or her.'

'No CCTV out here.'

'No… Damn…' She took a deep breath and grimaced. 'Look, I really hate having to ask, but could I use your phone? I need to find somewhere else to stay.'

The reality of her situation—and his—hit him then and his jaw tightened minutely. The only hotels available were no doubt less than salubrious and who knew how long it would take to find a vacancy? He knew what it was like to spend the night on the streets, cold and alone and afraid, and he wouldn't wish it on anyone. Venice was labyrinthine and not all of it was pretty enough to end up on a postcard.

He couldn't abandon her, no matter how much

he might wish to. Carla was here because of the challenge *he'd* issued and she was stuck because he'd allowed himself to be distracted and had lowered his guard. There was only one solution, and it didn't appeal in the slightest, but this was the price he had to pay for both his impulsivity and his carelessness.

'You'd better come home with me.'

Carla went very still, her gaze jerking to his, the horror he saw there and on her face suggesting she was as keen on the idea as he was. 'Oh, no, I really don't think that's necessary.'

'You'll be perfectly safe.'

She shook her head, her blonde hair shimmering beneath the twinkling lights distracting him for a moment. 'That's not it.'

'Then what is it?'

'I don't much like being dependent on anyone,' she said with a slight jut of her chin.

No, well, he could identify with that. 'I don't much like having anyone dependent on me, but we don't have a choice.'

She stiffened and something flashed in the depths of her eyes. 'I *always* have a choice.'

'As I said, it's high season. Everywhere decent will be full. There are areas of Venice you do not want to find yourself in, however briefly. It's nearly midnight and you must be wiped out. I know I am.' The exertions of today were taking their toll and his muscles were beginning to ache, so perhaps it was just as well he'd decided against seducing her, not that that was remotely relevant right now. 'But you're right. It *is* your choice. Here.'

Fishing his phone out of his jacket pocket, he put it on the table and pushed it towards her. For several long moments Carla just stared at it warily, as if it might be about to bite, and then she sighed and nudged it back towards him, her shoulders falling as she gave a brief nod.

'All right,' she said, looking impossibly weary and dejected, the smile she was trying to muster up weak. 'Thank you.'

'Things will look better in the morning,' he said, not having a clue why he felt the need to reassure her but for some reason really disliking the way the fight had drained from her.

'Of course they will.'

'Do you have a suitcase?'

'In the cloakroom.'

'Andiamo.'

While from the centre of his boat Rico navigated the canals that were a lot less busy than they'd been earlier, Carla sat at the back and used his phone to cancel her bank cards and her passport. Her phone had face recognition but she cancelled that too, just in case.

She was too preoccupied to take any notice of the tall, dark buildings as they slid quietly past, thinning out until they were far behind them. She wasn't in the mood to luxuriate in the inky depths of the night that enveloped her as they crossed the lagoon and the cool, fresh breeze that caressed her face, or admire Rico's skill and ease at the tiller of a vintage boat that was all beautiful varnished wood and sleek lines. She lacked the energy and enthusiasm to request a tour of his home, which she was sure would be huge and airy, based on the little of it she did see. She certainly didn't have time to contemplate the implications of having her most important material possessions stolen, practically from beneath her nose.

That, thanks to jet lag, came at three am.

Upon disembarkation at the jetty to which he'd tied the boat, Rico had grabbed her overnight bag and then alighted. He'd held out his hand to help her off, releasing her as soon as she'd done so, and headed up a path with an instruction to follow him tossed over his shoulder. Too battered by shock and weariness and the sizzling effect of his brief yet electrifying touch to do anything else, Carla had complied.

Once inside the house, he'd led her through a dimly lit but spacious hall, up a set of wide stone stairs and shown her to a guest suite that was probably the size of her entire flat. He'd then bade her a curt goodnight before turning on his heel and disappearing. She'd instantly flopped onto the bed and crashed out almost the minute her head hit the pillow.

Now, two hours later, she was wide awake, hot and sweaty, the sheets twisted around her from all the tossing and turning she'd been doing in a futile attempt to get back to sleep.

With a sigh of frustration, Carla disentangled herself and got up. She crossed the room, opened the doors that gave onto one of two balconies and stepped out into the darkness in the hope that cool night air might blast away the thumping of her head and quell the sick feeling that had started in the restaurant and had now spread into every cell of her body.

But the breeze that carried a welcome freshness and a hint of salt was no panacea for the churning of her stomach. The distant cries of seagulls couldn't drown out the rapid drum of her heartbeat. No distantly beautiful view of perhaps the world's most romantic city could sugarcoat the reality of her situation.

She was stranded, her plans derailed and her certainty about what she'd been doing shaken, her freedom and independence snatched away along with everything else. She was trapped, firstly by her arrogant assumption that the plan which seemed like such a good idea at lunchtime would work and secondly by her own stupidity.

How could she have let it happen? she wondered, swallowing down the wave of nausea rolling up her throat as she gazed across the lagoon at the odd sparkling light of the city far away. She knew how important her phone and her passport were and she knew the risks associated with leaving a handbag hanging on the back of a chair in a public space. As she'd so blithely and loftily told him, she'd travelled a lot.

Yet she'd been so thrown by Rico's effect on her, she'd failed to deploy her common sense. She hadn't given the security of her things a moment's thought at any point during dinner. She'd been reckless and unthinking and, worst of all, breathtakingly stupid, and as a result she was now entirely at the mercy of a man once again.

This time, the situation might be wholly her fault and not at all like the one in which she'd found herself as a teenager, but the emotions were all too familiar—the helplessness and the confusion, the vulnerability and the stripping away of her agency and her identity.

It had taken her months to rid herself of the chill that was rippling through her now, the self-doubt she could feel beginning to creep in and the tightness in her chest. She didn't like feeling this way when it wasn't who she was any more, and she hated even more the disturbing memories it invoked of a time when she'd been so naïve, so foolish.

Nor did she like being here, wherever here actually was, but Rico had been right—there hadn't been an alternative. It had occurred to her as she'd sat there staring at his phone, and burning up with regret and anger that she hadn't taken better care of hers, that she couldn't strike out on her own. She had no money and no ID. No hotel would take her in, even if she *had* managed to locate the details of the one she'd booked. She'd had to accept his offer, however nasty the taste it left in her mouth, however sick it made her feel.

But her enforced dependence on him wouldn't be for long, she assured herself, determinedly pushing the feelings and the memories away and pulling herself together. In the morning—well, later on, seeing as how it was already morning— she'd file a police report and investigate getting a new passport. She'd look at moving her flight and contact Georgie to ask her to get her locks changed, just to be on the safe side. She'd email her boss and let her know she wouldn't be in on Monday. Once she'd figured out how to get hold of some money she'd buy a phone and a few more clothes and then she'd find herself a hotel to stay in. Despite it being high season, surely the city would be less busy during the week than at the weekend.

She might be stranded but she would *not* be a victim, she told herself firmly as she gave her upper arms a quick rub before turning and heading back inside. Not again. *Never* again. She had resources. Somehow she would get herself out of this mess.

She needn't be troubled by her host. He'd hardly know she was here. She had plenty of things to be getting on with and presumably he did too. In the unlikely event their paths did cross, however, she'd be on her guard. She'd be polite but distant and think of some other way to encourage contact with Finn. She had no intention of giving up. Just because this plan had backfired badly didn't mean another would.

The one thing she definitely *wouldn't* be doing, she thought, climbing into bed and punching her pillow into shape, was indulging the attraction she felt for Rico, which just wouldn't seem to go away. She'd made that mistake with him once already and look what had become of it. Whatever else happened, she would *not* be making it again.

CHAPTER FIVE

IT WAS NEARING lunchtime when Carla finally emerged, not that Rico, who was in the kitchen throwing together something to eat, had been watching the clock.

In fact, he'd spent most of the morning ploughing up and down the pool in an effort to soothe and exercise his aching muscles. Despite taking painkillers that had knocked him out pretty much instantly, he hadn't slept well. For most of the night he'd thrashed about, his dreams filled with disjointed montages of his life on the streets as an adolescent, triggered by his continuing incredulity that he hadn't noticed the theft of Carla's handbag, the kind of dreams—or nightmares— that he hadn't had for years.

He wasn't in the best of moods and his acute awareness of his unexpected house guest wasn't helping. He didn't have people to stay. He didn't have people in his life full stop. He didn't want them and he certainly didn't need them. He might have thought he had once upon a time, and he might have thought he'd found the loyalty and family and sense of belonging he craved in the gang he'd joined when he was twelve, but he hadn't. The moment those hopes and expectations had been crushed was the moment he'd realised that he was on his own, and that the only person he could truly count on was himself.

All he needed to survive now was his isolation and his solitude, and he went to great lengths to protect them. It was the main reason he lived on an island in the lagoon instead of the *sestieri*. The fewer neighbours the better. He didn't want people nosing about in his business. Even his housekeeper, who came three times a week, went home at the end of each day she was there. Should he feel the need to entertain, he did so in the city.

This particular property of his might extend to fifty hectares, but Carla being in even a tiny part of it felt like a violation of his space, a further threat to his peace of mind, which was already in some turmoil. Her constant but unwelcome presence in his thoughts was frustrating. As if his dreams about his youth hadn't been disturbing enough on their own, up she'd popped in a number of them, teasing him with the spikiness that he found perversely attractive and tempting him to behave in a way that might be worth suffering a few aches and pains for.

Everything about the whole situation that he now found himself in was immensely irritating, and the realisation he'd come to mid-swim an hour ago made it additionally so. One unforeseen consequence of his reluctant chivalry was that if he wanted Carla gone, and gone fast, which he did, he'd have to be the one to facilitate it. Overnight, the private nature of his island, which he'd always considered a definite positive, had become a serious negative. She had things to do that could only be done in the city and he'd have to take her, which, he was forced to acknowledge with a grind of his teeth, was perhaps another example of acting in haste and repenting at leisure.

But he badly wanted his life back to the trouble-free, easy way it had been before he'd met Carla, before he'd seen the photo of Finn, before even the accident, and if that meant accompanying her every step of the way as she set about reclaiming what had been taken from her, to make sure she actually had the wherewithal to leave, then so be it.

He could resist the temptation she posed, he assured himself grimly, aware of a sudden shift in the air and bracing himself before turning to find her standing in the doorway, wearing a yellow sundress and flip-flops, looking like sunshine, her hair wet from the shower he would not be imagining her in ever. He could retain his grip on his control and shut down his response to her. If he ruthlessly stuck to the plan and deployed his usual devil-may-care approach to life, the one that had been strangely absent during the last twenty-four hours, everything would be fine.

'Good afternoon,' he said, fixing a lazy smile to his face and sounding pleasingly unmoved by her appearance.

'I didn't mean to disturb you.'

Far too late for that. 'You aren't. Come in.'

'I had no idea of the time,' she said, sliding her gaze to the clock on the wall above his head and giving a faint grimace as she stepped forward. 'I'm still recovering from my trip to Hong Kong, jet lag is a bitch.'

'Coffee?'

'That would be great, thank you.'

She came to a stop on the other side of the vast kitchen island unit and hopped up onto a stool. Resolutely not noticing how the movement tightened her dress around her chest, Rico turned his attention to taking a pot off the stove and poured the contents into a tiny espresso mug, which he then handed to her across the expanse of marble.

'Milk? Sugar?'

'No, thanks.' She took a sip and closed her eyes, while he watched her smile in satisfaction and for a moment forgot his name. 'Oh, that *is* good,' she said, which instantly had him imagining her breathing that exact same thing into his ear as he held her tight and moved inside her.

'Help yourself to brunch,' he muttered, with a quick cough to clear the hint of hoarseness from his voice and the unacceptably vivid image from his head.

'You cooked?'

'I can.' And well. Once upon a time, he'd sworn he would never go hungry again and he hadn't. 'However, today I merely assembled.'

Getting a ruthless grip on the imagination that had never troubled him before, Rico turned to the section of counter top where he'd been working and set about transferring plates of prosciutto and salami, mozzarella and Gorgonzola, and bowls of artichoke hearts, sun-dried tomatoes and olives to the island. With ciabatta and focaccia, in hindsight, it was rather a lot for two people but, 'I didn't know what you'd like.'

'I like it all,' she said with an apologetic wince as her stomach rumbled loudly. 'It looks delicious.'

She looked delicious, was the thought that shot into his head before he could stop it, and he wanted to devour her. 'Take a plate.'

'Thank you.' She did as he'd suggested and began filling it, only to pause a moment later. 'You know...' she said, then stopped.

'What?'

'Nothing.' She gave her head a quick shake, as if to clear it, and said instead, 'Thank you for putting me up last night.'

'You're welcome.'

'I'll be out of your hair just as soon as I can.'

The sooner the better, because what if, contrary to his expectations, he couldn't keep a lid on the attraction that instead of fading only seemed to be getting worse? What if he succumbed and lowered his defences and she went in for the kill? It didn't bear thinking about. 'I will help.'

'I can manage,' she said, flashing him a smile of her own, one that didn't quite reach her eyes and gave him the impression it was about as genuine as his.

'I don't doubt it.'

'So that's settled, then.'

If only. 'Not quite.'

Her green gaze narrowed slightly. 'How so?'

'Do you have any idea where you actually are?' he asked, thinking obviously not, judging by the faint frown that appeared on her forehead.

'Enlighten me.'

'Isola Santa Margherita.'

'Which is?'

'My island.'

She lowered the spoon she'd been using to her plate and stared at him. 'Your island.'

'Corretto.'

'Neighbours?'

'No.'

'Access to the city?'

'Boat.'

For a moment a shadow passed across her face and he thought he saw a shudder ripple through her but both were gone before he could be sure.

'There are taxis, I presume?'

He gave a brief nod and reminded himself that he needed to know as much about shadows or shudders as he did about smiles that weren't genuine, which was nothing. 'There are, but they're expensive and you have to book ahead. I and my boat, however, are free and entirely at your disposal.'

'Oh, I'm sure you must have lots to be getting on with,' she said, replacing the spoon in the bowl of olives and picking up a napkin.

'As a matter of fact, I don't. I'm supposed to be taking things easy.'

'Then you don't need to be ferrying me around.'

'It would be my pleasure,' he said with an easy coolness that matched hers. 'I'll take you anywhere you need to be.'

Quite frankly, Carla thought as she watched Rico embark on piling food onto his plate, she needed to be anywhere other than here, on a private island, cut off from the city, from people, from help. Anywhere other than having brunch with the man who'd presented her with a smorgasbord of deliciousness that had momentarily tempted her to divulge tales of the horrendous food she'd had to eat while growing up on a commune, which could well have wound up becoming a conversation about her instead of him and potentially led down a path she'd really rather not tread.

If only she hadn't hung about in the doorway to the kitchen, transfixed by the sight of him and rooted to the spot, but had instead got a grip and made herself scarce. If only she hadn't stood there, staring at his back, watching the muscles of his arms bunch and flex as he did whatever he was doing, struggling for breath and going weak at the knees while her temperature soared.

An effect of her still malfunctioning body clock? Probably not, but it was the excuse she'd decided upon and she was sticking to it. She was contemplating using it too as an explanation for actually considering accepting his suggestion to act as her taxi, despite her deep-seated desire to take care of herself.

Not that she really needed one.

If she applied clarity and reason to her thinking she'd see that this situation was nothing like the one it had reminded her of in the early hours of this morning. There was no malicious intent behind Rico's offer of help. No attempt to control her actions or her thoughts. No demand for anything in return. The island might be cut off but she wasn't. No one was stopping her from going anywhere.

She'd be better off focusing on the reality of today and not the memories of a decade ago, she told herself, adding a spoonful of artichoke hearts to her plate. Yes, she didn't want to be indebted to him and yes, it was bad enough that he'd had to rescue her in the first place, but surely the quicker she sorted everything out, the quicker she'd be home. With his means of transport and knowledge of the city, neither of which she had, Rico would definitely speed things up. She only understood enough Italian to be able to order off a menu. He'd be able to slice through the bureaucracy in a way that she simply couldn't.

Maybe she ought to learn to accept help without feeling as if she was somehow failing by not being able to handle things on her own. Just because she was capable didn't mean she had to be all the time. Maybe, occasionally, it would be a good idea to let someone else take the reins, on a practical level at any rate.

And, perhaps, he'd lend her some cash?

Carla had been financially independent for years, ever since she'd realised that having her own money and plenty of it would give her choice and freedom. She paid her credit card off in full every month. The only money she borrowed was for her mortgage. But even if she asked Georgie to send her some, with no ID she wouldn't be able to pick it up. Without her phone she couldn't access her digital wallet. However strong her motivations, however excellent her intentions, she had to be practical.

'OK, well, first of all,' she said, taking a great leap in her personal development by choosing to look forward not back, 'I need to go to the police station and report the theft of my things.'

'We can leave as soon as you're ready to go.'

'I also need to get a phone.'

'I thought you might,' he said, one corner of his mouth kicking up in a way that did sizzling things to her stomach which she could really do without. 'So I had this delivered this morning.' The model he slid in her direction she knew to be the latest of its kind and worth over a thousand euros. 'It's yours if you want it.'

See? she told herself while struggling to get a grip on the heat that was threatening to turn her into a puddle of lust. He wasn't trying to cut her off. Quite the opposite, in fact. 'On loan?'

'If you wish.'

'I insist.' She took a deep breath, then said,

'And on the subject of loans... I was wondering...'

'How much do you need?'

With a wince, she told him and he nodded. 'Not a problem.'

'I'll pay you back as soon as I can.'

'No hurry.'

There was every hurry, she thought as she popped an olive in her mouth and watched intrigued as Rico turned his attention to his own plate and began working through it with the same degree of focus he'd had last night. Because she might not disturb him any longer, but Rico, with his dark looks, cool confidence and decisiveness, certainly disturbed her. He was so attractive and so hard to resist on any number of levels. She had to take care not to let this practical help of his slide into something more dangerous where her emotions became involved and she became infatuated with him. The sooner she removed herself from his magnetising orbit and returned home, to her job, her friends, her *life*, the better.

But when it came to the actual police station visit itself, Carla was unexpectedly rather glad of his presence. As they approached and then pulled up at the jetty immediately in front of the entrance to the building, she welcomed the distraction provided by his proximity and solidity and didn't even bother to resist the temptation to keep the confusion and discomfort she'd felt at the intrusion, along with the fury and outrage and resentment at what had been done to her by those who'd ripped her away from her one true love. She remembered how it had all been brought up again at her abuser's trial, by which time she'd broken free of his malevolent influence and could see what had happened for the horror it really was, which had converted the resentment and fury into the shame and guilt that still faintly lingered even now, a decade later.

And today it was all too much. She was hot and she was tired. Her defences were weakened by the robbery and jet lag. She didn't want to be reminded of her abuser and what he'd done to her and how she'd facilitated it. Yet now it was all she could think of. The naïvety and the neediness she'd felt. The hundreds of emails they'd exchanged that contained an angst-ridden outpouring of her concerns, her worries, her hopes, her dreams. The intimate photos she'd sent and the innermost thoughts she'd shared.

The memories and the emotions whirled round her head faster and faster, as if she were on some kaleidoscopic, out-of-control merry-go-round. Her heart thundered as if trying to break her ribs. Her lungs tightened, her dress clinging to her body clammily. She couldn't breathe. Her head

glancing over and drinking in how very go[od]
looked in shorts that revealed the lower half
pair of very sexy legs, a T-shirt that moulde[d]
his muscles, and mirrored sunglasses.

The only other time she'd been anywhere ne[ar]
such an establishment was immediately afte[r]
she'd been rescued from the seedy east London
hotel she'd ended up in when she'd run away to
be with the man she'd thought she'd loved. The
occasion had been invasive and embarrassing and
horrible, she remembered, her pulse beginning to
race and her stomach churning as they alighted,
and, just in front of the arch through which she
and Rico had to proceed, her step faltered.

'Are you all right?' he asked, concern flickering in his gaze as he looked down at her.

She took a deep breath and fixed a smile to
her face. 'I'm fine,' she said, aiming for breezy
but not quite hitting it. 'Just not a huge fan of police stations. So let's get this over and done with,
shall we?'

She went ahead of him, and stepped out of the
bright sunlight and into the dark, busy station,
and it wasn't the same, obviously, but the uni-
forms and the noise and the musty, damp smell
acted like a trigger, and recollections of being in-
terviewed and inspected, stripped and swabbed,
suddenly slammed into her head.

In an instant she was awash with memories of

was swimming. Her limbs were turning to liquid. She felt as if she was about to throw up.

God, she wasn't going to faint, was she?

No. She couldn't be. She wasn't the type. She was strong and capable and a survivor. Yet her knees felt weirdly weak. Sweat was trickling down her back and her blood was pounding in her ears. She was hot, so very hot, and her vision was now blurring at the edges and her head was going all prickly.

The last thing she was aware of before her legs gave way was a strong arm whipping round her waist, a hard wall of muscle into which she collided, and then there was nothing but darkness.

Rico had experienced many, *many* things in his thirty-one years on the planet but having someone pass out on him was not one of them.

Thank God he'd caught Carla before she fell. Given the direction in which she'd listed, she'd most likely have hit her head on the corner of the very solid-looking table to her right and that might well have put her in hospital. Instead, she'd collapsed into the relative safety of his arms.

Ignoring the screaming protest of his body, he scooped her up in all her dead weight glory and barked out a series of orders that resulted in chairs being swiftly assembled into a row.

Now was not the time to notice how soft she

felt gathered up against him or how delicious she smelled. Nor was it the time to dwell on how well he knew this building, how often he'd spent the night here in these cells, having been caught earning money and later 'running errands' on the *sestieri*, a cocky and mouthy youth on the surface, a lost and petrified child beneath. Now was the time to lay her down to get her blood flowing in the right direction and procure the paperwork.

With what wasn't his most elegant of moves Rico set Carla down, pausing only to slide the strap of her dress that had fallen down up over her shoulder and absolutely not indulging in the temptation to linger.

Dio, the things he'd done, he thought darkly as he straightened and stalked over to the desk, the small crowd in front of it taking one look at the scar at his temple and the bump in his nose and parting like the waves. Willingly at first when he'd been desperate to prove himself and fit in but then increasingly less willingly when he'd gained the respect of his bosses and been asked to take on a bigger role and more responsibility, although by that point he'd been in so deep he hadn't been able to see a way out.

He hadn't been anywhere near this place in years. Not since that last time, when, at the age of sixteen, he'd been charged with crimes relating to money laundering. But it might as well have been yesterday. He could still recall how terrified he'd been despite the bravado. How slowly the hours had passed while he waited for his bosses to come and bail him out. How sick with devastation and disillusionment he'd felt when he'd realised no one was coming, that the loyalty he'd given them would not be repaid, and how unbelievably naïve and stupid he'd been to put his trust in people who'd dealt only in exploitation and had never known a code of honour.

But that was ancient history, he reminded himself with a clench of the jaw. On leaving the courtroom that day he'd slammed the door shut on everything that had happened to him between the death of his parents and turning his life around, and it no longer had the ability to affect him. Nothing on any level other than the purely physical did these days.

By the time he returned to Carla, forms in hand, she'd recovered and was sitting up, looking slightly dishevelled, slightly stunned, yet oddly, mystifyingly…adorable.

'What happened?' she asked, her question cutting through his bewilderment, since he'd never found anything adorable, oddly or otherwise, while the huskiness of her voice sent a jolt of awareness through him.

'You passed out.'

She stared at him. 'Seriously?'

'Yes,' he said curtly in an effort to pull himself together. 'You went out like a light.'

'Who *does* that these days?'

'You do, evidently. How are you feeling?'

'A bit odd,' she said, after thinking about it for a moment, and then added with a grimace, 'A lot mortified.'

'Should I call the paramedics?' he asked, the fact that he was asking a question instead of issuing an order and expecting it to be obeyed a further source of irritation. But if there was one thing he was beginning to realise about Carla, it was that she preferred to make her own decisions and didn't respond well to being told what to do, however well intentioned.

'No. I'm fine.'

He looked at her, caught the paleness of her face and the turmoil in the shimmering depths of her eyes, and frowned. 'You really don't like police stations, do you?'

'No,' she said with a faint shudder.

'Why not?'

She tensed. 'Does anyone?'

Well, he certainly didn't, which would have given them something in common had he ever been remotely interested in seeking such a thing with anyone. 'What made you faint?'

'The heat,' she said, and he might have believed her if she hadn't bitten her lip and shifted her gaze from his.

'It's not that hot.'

'Jet lag and lack of sleep on top of a stressful week and even more stressful weekend, then,' she said with a scowl. 'How would I know?'

Of course she knew. She wasn't the type to stumble. Or collapse. Besides, he'd felt the tension vibrating off her. He'd caught the turmoil in her expression the second before she'd fallen into his arms. But actually it didn't matter what he did or didn't believe. It was none of his business. He didn't need details. He was just here to facilitate her departure and get his life back. 'Do you need any help with the forms?'

'No, thank you.'

In the ten minutes it took her to fill in the details, Rico distracted himself by going through the seventy-five emails that had come in since they'd left the house, deleting or replying with single-minded focus and ruthless efficiency.

One unexpected disadvantage of working on his own with only back office support was that during the fortnight he'd spent in hospital being put back together while dosed up on morphine he'd been unable to operate his phone, let alone engage with the highly complex financial instruments he used to manage his funds. As a result he'd lost millions, which he was still in the process of recuperating.

The markets might be closed today but decisions still had to be made. Strategies had to be clarified. Requests had to be considered and, in the case of the email from one Alex Osborne of Osborne Investigations, who was apparently looking into his and Finn's biological family and was after details about him that he had either no intention of sharing or else didn't know, ignored.

Responding to or even engaging with the investigator, however briefly, would not help him in his quest to return his life to normal. It was bad enough that Finn kept popping into his head, triggered by Carla's revelation last night at dinner about how upset his brother had been by Rico's departure from his house.

The nonsensical guilt that came with these appearances was not something he appreciated. He doubted he could shed any light on anything anyway. He certainly didn't need to open the email that had come directly from this new-found brother of his. He wasn't interested in anything he might have to say. He wasn't interested in family full stop, and that was where this ended.

'That's it,' said Carla briskly, snapping him out of his dark, rumbling thoughts. 'I'm done.'

She stood up and swayed and Rico was on his feet in an instant.

'Steady,' he said, instinctively putting one hand on her shoulder, which he realised was a mistake the minute he did it. She tensed beneath his touch and her breath caught. Her gaze jerked to his, a flash of heat lighting the emerald-green depths of her eyes, which exploded a reciprocal burst of desire inside him before she shook his hand off at the exact same moment he snatched it away.

'Sit down,' he said curtly, resisting the urge to curl his hand into a fist to squeeze out the burn. 'I'll take them.'

For once she didn't protest but did as he suggested with alacrity, and by the time he returned with the report his hand had just about stopped tingling and the memory of the feel of her soft, smooth skin beneath his palm had just about gone.

'Want to get out of here?' he asked, looking down at her and noting with relief that she now displayed no hint of her reaction to his touch.

'Very much so,' she said coolly, clearly having decided, like him, to take the denial approach.

'Are you going to pass out again?'

'No.'

'Well, I don't know about you,' he muttered as they stepped outside out of darkness and into the light, 'but I could do with a drink.'

CHAPTER SIX

WHILE RICO ORDERED a couple of beers and pastries from the terrace of a cafe that had apparently been serving drinks from the same spot since 1750, Carla investigated the ways in which she might replace her stolen passport. It wasn't as complicated as she'd feared, helped by the fact that once upon a time she'd uploaded copies of her birth certificate, driving licence and passport to the cloud. Nevertheless, it still took far longer than it should have, in no small part because her thoughts kept drifting off and circling around what had just happened.

First of all, she couldn't believe she'd actually fainted like that. She'd never fainted before, ever. And to do so now, in front of a strong, controlled, insanely sexy man like Rico, well, embarrassing didn't begin to cover it. Nor did disappointment. She hated that the memories of a time she thought she'd dealt with had flooded back with such ease and such vividness.

Secondly, there was all the *contact* that had taken place. She could still feel the steel band of Rico's arm around her waist and the warm wall of hard muscle against which she'd been clasped moments before she lost consciousness. Her shoulder still burned with the imprint of his hand from when she'd stood up too fast and he'd steadied her. The high-voltage charge of electricity continued to zap through her blood and the flash of desire in his eyes was singed into her memory.

Most shocking of all was the realisation that Rico wasn't as immune to her as she'd assumed, that the attraction on his side hadn't gone and up until that moment he'd simply just been very good at hiding it.

Well, whatever.

None of it made a scrap of difference to how she proceeded, Carla told herself sternly as she clicked on the submit button and a moment later received a confirmation email. In a couple of days she'd be gone and this little blip in her otherwise well-ordered, smoothly running life would be over.

'So I've ordered an emergency travel document,' she said, mightily relieved to have gained at least a modicum of control of the situation. 'It'll be ready at the British Consulate in Milan on Wednesday.'

'Wednesday?'

At the hint of censure in Rico's voice she glanced up at him to find him frowning, the expression on his face dark and disapproving, which was odd, since the machinations of bureaucracy were hardly anything to do with her. 'It takes two working days, minimum.'

'Give me a minute.'

He put down his bottle of beer, took out his phone and a minute later was rattling away in Italian. Carla listened, trying not to stare at his mouth, which was difficult when it was such a beautiful mouth producing such a beautiful language in deep, rich, spine-tingling tones, and idly pondered taking lessons. Not that she was planning to return any time soon, of course, and it wasn't as if she wanted a memento of her time here, but—

'Your new passport will be ready tomorrow.'

Jolted out of her musings, she wrenched her gaze from his mouth to his eyes. An actual passport? Tomorrow? Oh. Right. Well. That was good. 'How did you do that?'

'I'm owed a favour.'

By the British Consulate? Who was he? And why was she feeling ever so slightly piqued that he was as keen to see her leave as she was to go? That made no sense. She ought to be delighted they were on the same page, even if it did truncate the amount of time she had to achieve her goal.

'Are you owed enough of a favour to have it couriered here?' she asked, deciding to attribute that particular anomaly to jet lag, along with everything else.

'Unfortunately not. You need to pick it up in person.'

So checking out trains was another thing she was going to have to do as well as changing her flight to Tuesday morning and booking a hotel.

'Never mind,' she said, thinking that at least she wouldn't have to wash out her underwear any longer than was necessary. She'd only packed for an overnight stay and she hadn't been looking forward to having to put on damp knickers. 'Thank you, anyway.'

'You can continue to stay with me until you leave. I'll take you to Milan in the morning.'

What? No. No way.

'And before you object,' he added when she automatically opened her mouth to do exactly that, 'it is not an inconvenience. I am aware that you are extremely capable and can handle this on your own. I know you're no damsel in distress and I have no intention of telling you what to do, or preventing you from doing anything you want to do, if you insist upon it. It's simply an efficient use of resources and makes the most sense. That is all.'

Hmm. Carla didn't know about that. In her opinion, staying with Rico would mean approximately thirty-six more hours of trying to keep a lid on the attraction that instead of dissipating seemed to be growing in intensity. It would mean spending time with him, which would result in the kind of stress and discomfort that did not appeal. It would mean further reliance on someone who wasn't her, and worse, on a *man*.

On the other hand, it *would* provide an opportunity to restart her temporarily derailed mission to change his mind about meeting Finn. Earlier, she'd opened an email from Georgie, in which her best friend had asked how she was getting on and whether she'd made any progress. The deluge of guilt and shame she'd felt at the realisation that she'd allowed her own issues to take over had prevented her from replying. She didn't want to have to admit that she hadn't made very much progress at all. She didn't want to have to confess to all the reasons why.

Now was the chance to get back on track and rectify that. If she accepted his proposal and installed herself in his house, Rico would be a captive audience. She'd give him no option but to talk. She might not have much time, but in the course of her career she'd achieved a lot more with less, and here, failure was not an option. This time, nothing was going to get in her way. Her focus would remain unshakeable.

She'd put her plan into action the minute they returned to his island. He wouldn't know what had hit him. She'd start with his house and go from there. You could tell a lot about a person from the place they called home. And then she'd move on to everything else she wanted to know, such as why he'd really walked out of Finn's study yesterday lunchtime and what exactly he had against police stations. She'd noticed the tension that had radiated off him when she'd been filling in the forms. It hinted at dark secrets she badly wanted to uncover. For the job she was here to do, naturally.

Why he obviously now had no intention of acting on the attraction he still felt for her was not something she needed to know, any more than why he affected her so fiercely. The mission was her number one priority. It was the only thing that mattered now, so she'd be a fool and a coward not to accept his offer, not to mention an appalling best friend, and she hoped she was no longer any of those things.

'Thank you,' she said with a nod, ignoring the flutter of misgiving that nevertheless flickered deep inside her. 'That would be great.'

* * *

What Rico was doing inviting Carla to stay, to invade his space and shatter his privacy, he had no idea. He'd caught the flare of triumphant satisfaction in her eyes while she'd been considering what best to do. He knew what she was going to attempt. Hadn't he recognised her tenacity and her resourcefulness and decided to have nothing to do with her precisely because she might slip beneath his guard? By taking her back to his home, by exposing himself to the barrage of prying questions that was undoubtedly coming his way, wasn't he potentially not just lowering his guard but also quite possibly tossing it aside altogether?

Rico had been taking risks from the moment he'd woken up to the harsh realities of life at the age of sixteen and discovered he cared about absolutely nothing. He had no responsibilities, was accountable to no one, and therefore had zero to lose. So why shouldn't he pursue the thrill his reckless actions gave him, especially when they unfailingly turned out well?

Telling Carla she could continue to stay with him, however, was reckless beyond belief, a risk too great even for him to take. He knew that. It destabilised the status quo. It threatened the very essence of who he was. So why had his instincts, the ones he'd never yet had cause to doubt, prodded him to do it? Why did inviting Carla into his space, regardless of what she might do with it, feel so right?

Steering the boat towards the jetty, Rico eased off on the throttle and tossed a buoy over the side. The boat bumped gently against the wood, jarring the thoughts knocking around his head, and he threw a loop of rope over the mooring post.

Perhaps he was overthinking this, he thought grimly as Carla grabbed the replacement bag she'd bought and hopped off before he could even think about offering her a hand, which was a relief. Where was the danger really? If she started bombarding him with questions about himself and reasons why he should establish proper contact with his brother he'd be ready. If she decided to get personal, he could choose what to reveal and what to keep secret. He'd been doing it for years. And as for the scorching desire he felt for her, his will power was strong and she'd be gone soon enough.

Shaking off the unease and focusing on the eminently sensible way he was going to handle the next thirty-six hours, Rico stepped off the boat and set off up the cypress tree-lined path that led to the house.

'What made you choose to live here instead of the city?' she asked, falling in beside him.

'It's cool in the heat of the summer,' he replied, and it was partly the truth. She didn't need to know about his craving for space, clean air and greenery after calling the dirty urban streets home for too long. 'There's plenty of room for the pool. Plus you can't land a helicopter in the city.'

'I can see how that would be inconvenient.'

'You'll see just how convenient it is tomorrow when I take you to Milan.'

'We're going by helicopter?'

'Fastest way to get there.'

'Speed is good.'

Not always. He could think of plenty of occasions when slow was better. But now wasn't one of them, so he upped his pace, as uncomfortably aware of Carla hot on his heels as he was of the sharp complaint of his muscles.

'We'll leave at eight.'

'I'll change my flight to Tuesday morning,' she said with a slight breathlessness that he ruthlessly ignored. 'Just in case there's any delay tomorrow.'

'I'll take you to the airport.'

'That would be appreciated.'

'It's no problem at all.'

They continued in silence for a moment and then she said, 'So if I'm going to be staying here for a little while longer, would you show me around? I wouldn't want to get lost and wind up somewhere I shouldn't.'

'Now?'

'Unless you have somewhere else to be. The standard tour will do.'

'There is no standard tour,' he said, faintly disturbed about the thought of her nosing around his home even though it was too late for regrets.

'The premium one, then.'

'There's never been a tour of any kind.'

'Don't tell me I'm your first house guest.'

'All right, I won't,' he said, coming to a stop at the front door and glancing at her as he pushed his sunglasses onto his head then fished his keys from the pocket of his shorts.

Her eyes widened as she reached the obvious conclusion. 'Am I?'

'As I told you, I value my privacy.'

'My lips will remain sealed.'

As if on cue, his gaze dropped to her mouth and the world seemed to stop, keys, tours, privacy forgotten and in their place nothing but a drumming need that drowned out everything but the two of them.

He wanted to step forward, plant his hands on her shoulders and press her up against the warm, solid oak of the door. He wanted to lower his head to hers and cover her mouth with his and kiss her until neither of them could think straight.

He could almost feel her arms around his neck, her fingers tangling in his hair. He could imagine all too clearly her arching her back to plaster herself against him and the soft, sighing gasps she might emit.

She was standing so close he wouldn't even have to make much of a move. One step and he could yield to the hot, powerful desire surging through him. One step and she'd be in his arms and kissing him back because he just knew the same thing was running through her mind. She'd gone very still and her smile was fading. She was as transfixed by his mouth as he was by hers and a flush was appearing on her cheeks.

She wanted him as much as he wanted her, only this time, he realised while his body hardened and throbbed, she wasn't rejecting it. This time she wasn't pulling back. This time she was actually leaning towards him, her eyes darkening with desire that he badly wanted to stoke.

But to act on the attraction that still burned between them could expose him to her perceptiveness and uncanny insight and there was no way in hell he was going to allow that to happen. Besides, he had a plan for how to handle her—a sensible one, which was remarkable for a man who thrived on recklessness—and he had every intention of sticking to it.

The house, he reminded himself, taking a mental step back from the brink of insanity and clearing both his throat and his head. That was what she'd asked him about. The house.

Swiftly putting some distance between them, he turned to unlock the door. 'The villa was originally built by a seventeenth-century industrialist as a summer retreat,' he said, striding out of the dazzling, reason-wrecking heat and into the cool, calm interior.

'What?'

He glanced over his shoulder, the slight huskiness to her voice grating over his nerve-endings, and he noticed that she was looking a little flustered, which was only fair when she'd had a similarly devastating effect on him. 'You asked about the house.'

'Right,' she said, giving herself a quick shake and following him in, composure unfortunately restored. 'Yes. So how long have you lived here?'

'Since the renovations were completed five years ago.'

'And before that?'

'Milan.'

'What were you doing there?'

Grafting, mainly. Working sixteen-hour days and moving quickly up the ranks. Making the most of the opportunity he'd been given to shed his past and turn his life around. 'Building my career.'

'Do you live here permanently?' she asked as he led her through the huge drawing room, the snug, the study and the dining room that could host supper for twenty, looking at the space through a visitor's eyes and wondering what she thought, even though her opinion really didn't matter. With his wealth he could have bought any number of lavish palaces, but he didn't need opulence. He just needed space and light and comfort.

'I have places elsewhere,' he said. 'But this is my home.'

'It's beautiful,' she said, stopping at the base of a set of wide stone steps that went up and round, while he wondered what to do with the strange kick of pleasure he felt at the approval he'd told himself he didn't want. 'Light and airy but very, *very* minimalist.'

'Thank you.'

'It wasn't necessarily a compliment.'

'Oh?'

'Where are all your things?'

He frowned, disquiet zigzagging through him. 'What things?'

'Photos, knick-knacks, trinkets, mementos. You know, the stuff and clutter a person generally accumulates as they go through life.'

'I don't have any.'

Her eyebrows lifted and she stared at him in astonishment. 'None?'

'I prefer to look forward, not back.'

'So you hang on to *nothing*?'

'I don't see the point.'

'I guess it saves on the dusting.'

It saved on the navel-gazing. It prevented the stirring up of memories of times he'd long since blocked out, and unwanted, unnecessary emotional ties. It facilitated a life free of burden and responsibility. But he'd been right in his initial assessment of her. She *did* see far too much. Which meant he had to be exceptionally careful about what else he allowed her access to.

'What's up there?'

'My bedroom suite.'

For a moment, his words hung between them, charging the sudden silence with crackling static, while their gazes locked as if held by some invisible unbreakable thread, and then, with a swallow and a shaky laugh, she said, 'I probably don't need to see that.'

'No,' he agreed with an evenness that belied the fierce heat suddenly whipping around inside him, making him harden and ache. 'You don't.'

And there was no 'probably' about it. It was bad enough that she could roam around the communal areas of the house. Bad enough that he could envisage her walking up the stairs ahead of him, looking over her shoulder with heat and desire in her mesmerising green gaze and then gliding into his room, shedding her clothes and pulling him down with her onto his bed. Under no circumstances was she checking out his suite just in case she 'got lost and wound up somewhere she shouldn't'.

Instead, having hauled his body back under control, he took her up another set of stairs at the opposite side of the hall that led to the guest rooms, all four of them, one of which was temporarily hers, which again, did not need to be seen by either of them, and then back down, through a set of French windows and into the garden.

'The gym is a recent addition,' he said, stalking towards the studio and opening the door onto a vast room furnished with state-of-the-art equipment, where he'd spent much time slowly regaining his strength.

'Installed after your accident?'

'Yes.'

'You said a BASE jump went wrong.'

'That's right.'

'What led to the bad landing?' she asked, weaving between the machines, inspecting them with interest as she went.

Annoyingly unable to take his eyes off her, Rico leaned against the wall and jammed his hands in his pockets. 'The jump itself was fine,' he said, remembering the thunder of nerves and anticipation as he'd stepped off the top of a snow-capped mountain that rose up two thousand metres above sea level and begun soaring through jagged cliffs, high on speed and adrenaline and invincibility. 'But, coming in to land, a gust of wind caught my wingsuit and blew me off course. I over-adjusted and slammed into a tree, and from there I crashed to the ground.'

The disbelief had almost been as great as the pain, he recalled, still unable to fully credit what had happened. He'd been BASE jumping for years, thriving on the exhilaration, taking ever-increasing risks in this as with everything he did, because why not?

The few accidents he'd had had been expected and minor. Until this one, which had seen him airlifted to hospital in Courmayeur, where he'd endured hours of complex surgery, followed by a stint at a clinic back home in Venice and then a gruelling physiotherapy programme that technically he was still supposed to be in the middle of.

'A rookie mistake?'

'I have a thousand skydives and two hundred BASE jumps under my belt,' he said. 'It's simply one of the most dangerous sports you can do and on this occasion I was unlucky.'

The look she threw him was disconcertingly shrewd. 'Is the danger the attraction?'

'Yes.'

'You're a risk-taker.'

'I am. Are you?'

She gave her head a shake. 'Quite the opposite.

I like things planned, organised and well thought through. I like control.'

'Yet you work in crisis management and damage limitation, where the unexpected is the norm.'

'True,' she admitted, 'but the unexpectedness is expected. Will you go back to doing it?'

'BASE jumping? No,' he said, realising, once his brain had caught up with his mouth, that it was true. Which was odd. Because why would he want to give it up? Yes, he'd been injured, but he'd been injured before, albeit not quite so severely, and been back in the saddle as soon as he could. What was different about this time? And why was his chest tight and his pulse fast?

'What will you do instead?'

'I don't know,' he admitted uneasily, apparently unable to answer anything right now.

'Doesn't it get a bit lonely, rattling around here on your own?'

'No.'

'You should get a pet.'

The thought of it sent a shudder through him. 'I don't think so.'

'Why not?'

Because he needed attachments like a hole in the head. Because he preferred to move through life alone and apart, and that precluded animals. 'I don't want one.'

'Why not?'

'What business is it of yours?'

'I'm seeing a theme.'

'What kind of a theme?' he asked, a strange sense of apprehension beginning to trickle though him.

'No neighbours, no pets, no clutter, no attachments of any kind. You don't just live on an island, Rico, you *are* an island. So was that why you left Finn's study?' she asked with a tilt of her head. 'Did the thought of potential attachment spook you?'

'Not at all,' he said easily, although how close she was to the truth was making him sweat. 'I merely remembered I had somewhere else to be.'

'Here?'

'Precisely. And now, if you'll excuse me, I'm going for a swim.'

CHAPTER SEVEN

AS IF A swim was going to succeed in putting her off, thought Carla, watching Rico stalk out of the gym as if he had wolves snapping at his heels.

She'd been right in her belief that one could discover a lot from exploring another person's house. In Rico's case, she'd indirectly learned that exiting a conversation when it touched a nerve was what he did, and it revealed more than she suspected he was aware of. It gave her points to note and avenues to pursue, such as why he moved through life like a ghost, living in such isolation, even if the isolation was splendid, as indeed it was.

The walls throughout his house were a soft off-white, the floors made up of great slabs of travertine covered with huge, ancient earth-toned rugs. Fine voile hung at the open windows and fluttered in the breeze. The furniture that was wood gleamed, while the sofas and chairs looked sumptuous and inviting.

But the stark absence of personal effects intrigued her. Even the kitchen, which was filled with shiny gadgetry and utensils that obviously weren't simply for show, bordered on the clinical. And as for his study, a room in which presumably he spent much of his time, well, she'd never seen such order. His desk was bare apart from three massive monitors and a telephone, and not a file was out of place on the floor-to-ceiling shelves that lined one wall.

Did Rico have a place elsewhere crammed to the rafters with all his things? If he didn't, and this was him, was there really nothing and no one in his past that he wanted to hang on to, to remember? How sad and lonely his life must be with no family and no friends, she thought, feeling a tug on her heartstrings even though how he lived was no concern of hers.

But if he needed breathing space, she was more than happy to let him have it. She knew when to push and when to retreat. How to plant the seed of suggestion and wait for it to take root. Not that she had a lot of time to get anything to take root, but it gave her a bit of breathing space too, which she badly needed after what had happened at his front door when he'd gone very still, his mesmerising blue eyes darkening to indigo and his expression unfathomable as he looked at her with heart-thumping intensity.

She'd had the crazy notion that he'd been contemplating kissing her and even more crazily, for one split second, she'd actually hoped he would, instinctively softening and leaning in and preparing herself for fireworks until he'd suddenly drawn back, leaving her feeling mortified and rattled.

This feeling of being constantly unsettled and on edge was unacceptable, she told herself for the thousandth time as she made her way to her room to send Georgie an email giving her a temporary number and an update, and to arrange some annual leave for next week. As was the longing to know what Rico's bedroom looked like, and not just because perhaps *that* was where he stashed all his things. She did not need to know anything about his bedroom or how exciting it would be to kiss him.

The only interest she had in his attitude to risk was that it was another thing to investigate and report back to Finn. An analysis of how different it was to hers was not required, any more than was the kick of appreciation she'd felt in the pit of her stomach when she'd realised that he recognised her ability and need to take care of herself.

She would not be sidling across her room to the balcony that overlooked the terraces to check out the splash she'd just heard that indicated a gorgeous man might now be in the pool, scything slickly through the water while wearing virtually nothing. She would not be contemplating how deliciously tanned his skin might be, how powerfully he might move or whether the well-honed definition of his muscles was limited to his arms.

Time was marching on and she had a job to do, and she would concentrate one hundred per cent on that.

Rico tended to do much of his strategising while pounding up and down his pool, and the swim he'd just taken was no exception. As the rhythmic strokes cleared his head of the tangle of unanswerable questions Carla had stirred up, and his body of the excruciating tension that had been gripping him, he'd had something of an epiphany. Not about the shift in his attitude towards BASE jumping—that was still clear as mud—but about how to handle Carla and her continued attempts to prise information out of him.

One excellent way of putting a stop to it, it had occurred him as he'd flip turned and switched from crawl to butterfly, would be to divert the focus of conversation from him to her instead. He had no interest in finding anything out about her, of course, but if she was talking about herself she wouldn't be able to interrogate him. She'd be too busy picking and choosing her own answers, the way she had at dinner last night and the police station earlier.

He might be out of practice when it came to conversation, while she was anything but, but how challenging could it be to turn her questions back on her? How hard would it be to drum up some of his own that might just wrong-foot her the way hers did him?

It was an approach that would require focus and caution, he thought with a stab of satisfaction and relief at finally having come up with a way of taking back the upper hand, but it would get him through the hours until she left, certainly through the supper he was about to start preparing, and it was a solid one.

Determined to concentrate on the job she'd come to do and not get distracted once again by the subject of her investigations, Carla walked into the kitchen and didn't even break stride at the unexpectedly sexy sight of a big, handsome man standing at the island and pouring boiling water over a couple of tomatoes in a bowl.

'How was your swim?' she said, noting when he glanced up at her that there was a gleam to his eye that she'd never seen before, which was both shiveringly unsettling and unnecessarily intriguing.

'Refreshing,' he said with the easy-going smile that she'd learned concealed so much. 'Wine?'

'Thank you.'

He poured her a glass of something pale and cold and—she took a sip—utterly delicious. 'Is there anything I can do to help?'

'You can get the clams from the fridge.'

Reminding herself to focus, which was hard when she could feel his eyes burning into her back, Carla put down her glass and walked over to the appliance he'd indicated and opened the door.

'Wow,' she said, staring at the shelves that were crammed with more food than she'd ever seen in one place outside a supermarket. 'You have one very well-stocked fridge.'

'I like to eat.'

Yet there wasn't a spare ounce on him. She'd felt him when she'd fainted into his arms. Nothing but warm, solid muscle… 'So I've noticed,' she said, hauling her recalcitrant thoughts back on track with more effort than she'd have liked.

'Oh?'

'Last night,' she said, locating the box of clams and taking it out. 'At the restaurant. You ate as though you were afraid that if you put your fork down for even a second someone would whip your plate away.'

'The food there is good and I'd missed lunch.'

Hmm. 'It seemed like more than that. And you did it again at brunch today.'

'Do you cook?'

'I never learned.'

'Why not?'

'Work's always been crazily busy,' she said, as an image of her fridge, which generally contained milk, ready meals and not a lot else, slid through her mind. 'I've been putting in fourteen-hour days for years. That doesn't leave a lot of time for haute cuisine.'

'What were you doing in Hong Kong?'

'Dealing with a crisis and a CEO who didn't believe there was one.'

'I imagine you eventually persuaded him to see things your way.'

'Of course,' she said with a quick grin that drew his gaze to her mouth and for the briefest of moments stopped time.

'You really enjoy what you do, don't you?'

'Very much.'

'Why?'

'I like solving problems and fixing things. I also love a challenge,' she said with a pointed look in his direction, which was rather wasted, since he'd switched his attention to peeling a clove of garlic. 'Do *you* like what *you* do?'

'Yes.'

'How did you get into fund management?'

'I have a talent for numbers and a drive to make money,' he said, then added, 'You should be careful you don't burn out.'

What was it to him? she wondered, as bewildered by his concern as she was by the rogue flood of warmth she felt in response to it. Why did he care whether she burned out or not? And hadn't they been talking about him in the first place?

Ah.

She saw what he was doing, she thought as the warmth fled and strangely cold realisation struck. He was trying to manipulate the conversation. Well, that was fine. At least she'd recognised it. And now she had, she could use it. This whole exercise was supposed to be about her extracting information from him, not vice versa, but perhaps things would move more efficiently if she went along with his plan. She need give away nothing of significance. She hadn't so far and now she was on her guard, she wouldn't. There'd be no more warmth stealing through her at anything he might say and there'd be no more grins, quick or otherwise.

'And that's why I've taken next week off,' she said, taking a sip of her drink and noting a fraction more acidity than she had before.

'What are you going to do?'

'I have no idea. Sleep probably. I haven't had a

break in months. I suppose I could learn to cook. I might even take up Italian. And, talking of languages, how come your English is so good?'

'It's the language of business and I have an ear for it.'

His reply was too quick and too smooth, and undoubtedly only partly the truth. 'You understand nuance and inference and your accent is almost flawless. That's quite an ear.'

'*Grazie,*' he said, taking a knife to the garlic and slicing it with impressive deftness.

'Where were you raised?'

'Mestre. Across the lagoon, on the mainland. You?'

'On a series of communes in various corners of the UK.'

'Not much opportunity for haute cuisine there, I imagine,' he said with a smile that bounced off her defences.

'None whatsoever. We mainly survived on lentils and vegetables.'

'Siblings?'

'No.'

'Parents?'

'Yes.'

'Do they still live on a commune?'

'Yes.'

'Are you certain?'

'Why wouldn't I be?'

'You don't make time for them.'

Why would he think such a thing? she wondered for a moment before recalling their conversation last night in the restaurant. 'I never said that.'

'You didn't need to.'

'All right,' she admitted, faintly thrown by the fact that he'd remembered such a tiny detail too. 'I don't see them all that often. It's complicated. Are yours still on the mainland?'

'Mine died in a car crash when I was ten.'

A silence fell at that, and despite her attempts to remain coolly aloof Carla couldn't help but be affected. God, how awful, she thought, her chest squeezing and her stomach tightening. How tragic. He'd been so young. How did something like that affect the boy and then the man? How had it changed him? She couldn't imagine being so wholly on her own. After what had happened to her, her parents had felt so guilty and regretful that they'd gone from borderline negligent to smothering, and yes, their relationship was strained because of it but at least they were around.

'I'm so sorry,' she said with woeful inadequacy.

He gave a shrug. 'It was a long time ago.'

'Finn lost his mother at the age of ten, too.'

'And what were *you* doing at the age of ten, Carla?' he countered, neatly avoiding the point.

Trying to get her parents' attention, mostly, she thought, remembering how she'd constantly played up at the various schools she'd attended. Figuring out how to persuade them to stay in one place long enough for her to make friends. 'I don't know,' she said, shifting on her stool to ease the stab of age-old pain and disappointment. 'Listening to music and hanging out with the other kids on the communes, I guess.'

The look he gave her was disconcertingly shrewd. 'Why do I get the feeling that isn't all?'

'I truly can't imagine,' she said before deciding to engage in a bit of conversational whiplash of her own. 'Did you know you were adopted?'

'It was never a secret. There was some effort to locate my birth parents after the death of my adoptive ones.'

'But they weren't found.'

'No.'

'Weren't you ever interested in carrying on the search?'

'No.'

'Why not?'

'I discovered I preferred being on my own.'

'You aren't any more.'

He didn't respond to that, just slid the garlic from the board into the sizzling oil in the pan, and then gave it a toss, which made her think it could be time to shake things up on the conversational

front too. She had to at least *try* and make him
see reason about the family he could have now.

'Did you know you were born in Argentina?'
she asked, dismissing the guilty feeling she might
nevertheless be crossing a line because for Georgie and Finn there never would be a line.

'No.'

'Then you can't know that there are three of
you.'

'What do you mean?'

'You're one of three. There's you and Finn and
one other. You're triplets. All boys.'

The only indication that what she'd said had
had any impact at all was a tiny pause in his stirring of the garlic. 'Who's the third?' he asked
after a beat of thundering silence.

'No one knows.'

'He hasn't been found?'

'Not yet. You may be able to help.'

'I couldn't even if I wanted to.'

'Which you don't.'

'No.'

'Why not?'

'I'm not interested.'

But Rico was lying. He'd resumed his methodical stirring of the garlic but she could tell by the
tension gripping his body and the muscle ticking
in his jaw. He *was* interested and it gave her the

encouragement to persist. 'What did you think when you first saw Finn's photo?'

'I was surprised.'

'That's it?' she said. 'No lightning bolt of recognition? No sense of… I don't know…everything suddenly falling into place or something?'

'Absolutely not.'

'Well, *something* drove you to seek him out in his own home,' she said, beginning to feel a bit riled at the way he was deliberately blocking her at every possible point yet determined not to give up. 'So I think you're not only lying to me, but also to yourself.'

'You don't know me well enough to make that kind of judgement,' he said, the even tone of his words not quite disguising the warning note she could hear, telling her to retreat this minute.

'You're generous with your time and your resources,' she countered, ignoring it. 'You like police stations as little as I do. You back off when conversation gets too close. You're a risk-taker and a thrill-seeker and you have an unusual relationship with food. And lastly, you're attracted to me yet you don't want to be, which is odd when only yesterday lunchtime you were asking me out.'

'A mistake.'

'Evidently.'

'And the only reason I've been helping you is

to ensure you leave Venice just as soon as is humanly possible.'

Okay. Well. 'What I *do* know,' she said, absolutely refusing to take offence at those last two points of his, since she didn't care what he thought of her, 'is that no man is an island, not even you, Rico. Everyone needs someone and you have the very best of a someone. You have a brother. I can't understand why you wouldn't be moving heaven and earth to make up for lost time.'

'And I can't understand why you're so desperate for me to meet Finn,' he said bluntly. 'You came to *Venice*, Carla. What is your interest in this?'

'I told you,' she said, refusing to be intimidated by the darkening of his expression. 'Georgie is like family to me.'

'Why?'

'We've been through a lot together.'

'Such as?'

She wasn't ready to tell him. She'd never be ready to tell him. 'We're not talking about me.'

His eyes glittered. 'I think we should start.'

'There's no point.'

'There's every point. Why don't you see your parents, Carla?'

'Why don't you like police stations?' she shot back.

His jaw tightened. 'Why do you work so hard? What are you running from?'

'Why have you decided to shut yourself off from everyone and everything? What are *you* running from?'

'Nothing.'

'I don't believe you.'

'That's not my problem.'

'So what *is* your problem?' she asked, her blood heating to a simmer.

'You are.'

'Then you should have let me stay in a hotel.'

'I know.'

'Why didn't you?'

'I don't know,' he said roughly. 'Maybe I didn't want you to come to any harm by fainting again and falling into a canal. Maybe I wanted to uncover your secrets the way you're so determined to hunt down mine. Maybe for some inexplicable reason I felt responsible for you.'

For a moment a flame of pleasure flickered into life inside her but she swiftly extinguished it because none of that could be true. If it was it would mean she was somehow beginning to matter to him, which couldn't be the case when he was detachment personified. And the very idea of him being responsible for her was ridiculous. 'Distracting me won't work.'

'Then what will?' he said, putting down the spoon and stalking round to her side of the island, his eyes glittering and his shoulders rigid. 'What *will* it take to stop you talking?'

She could think of something. She could think of lots of things, all of them accelerating her pulse and heating the simmer to a boil. He could give her a smile—a real one—that would drain the blood from her head and suck the breath from her lungs. He could pulverise her thoughts with a touch and stop her mouth with a kiss, and he would barely have to even try.

'Agreement to go and see Finn,' she said a bit breathlessly, struggling to block out the images of him doing all of that.

'That's not going to happen.'

'Answers, then.'

'You're getting them,' he said softly, taking one step closer to her, trapping her against the island and looming over her in a way that should have felt threatening and should have triggered a need to escape but was instead having the opposite effect.

'Not the ones I want.'

'So what *do* you want, Carla?'

Something she really shouldn't but was finding it increasingly hard to resist, she thought, burning up in response to his size and proximity. Because Rico might be a threat to her self-control and an attack on her defences, but right here, right now, with her thoughts spinning and her body on fire, she couldn't quite remember why.

All she knew was that she wanted him and he wanted her. Heat flared in the inky blue depths of his glittering eyes. She could feel the tightly leashed power and tension tightening his body. Her heart thundered. Her breath hitched. The intensity with which he was looking at her was stealing her wits and stoking the desire whipping around inside her and she didn't even care.

'You know what I want,' she said, giving him the option to interpret her words in one of two ways, trying to tell herself she was still talking about Rico meeting Finn but actually meaning she wanted *him*, and practically erupting with excitement when he got it.

Whether it was the way she'd jutted her chin up in silent challenge or whether he was equally at the mercy of the attraction that flared between them and could no longer deny, she neither knew nor cared. He took her in his arms and with a muffled curse brought his mouth down on hers and all that mattered then was kissing him back as fiercely as he was kissing her.

With a moan she wrapped her arms around his neck and wound her fingers through his hair, which was as thick and soft as she'd imagined, and pressed herself so close that there was barely an inch of her that wasn't touching him. The heat and skill of his mouth, his lips, his tongue sent shock waves of desire shooting through her, fogging her brain and focusing all her attention on him and what he was doing to her.

She moaned again and he tightened his hold on her, deepening the kiss as he put his hands on her waist and lifted her onto the island as if she weighed nothing. She instinctively opened her legs and he stepped between them, and she could feel the thick, hard length of his erection pressing against the spot that was aching and desperate.

She tilted her hips to increase the pressure and writhed against him, needing him closer, inside her, while his hands were in her hair, on her back, large and warm against her body, holding her in place, scorching through the thin fabric of her dress.

With a harsh groan he moved his mouth to her neck, to the sensitive spot beneath her ear, and a hand to her breast, which instantly tingled and tightened and made her wish there was no material in the way either on her or him.

Suddenly desperate to discover what she'd denied herself by not checking him out in the pool earlier, she tugged at his T-shirt, he reared back and pulled it over his head, and there was his chest in all its naked glory. Tanned. Muscled.

And scarred.

A small brown circle lay just above his heart

and another on his opposite shoulder. A thin white mark cut a jagged line through the smattering of fine dark hair at the bottom of his ribcage.

But before she had time to even think about what they could be or what they might mean, he'd leaned forwards and bent his head for another scorching kiss and all she could focus on was the desire hammering around inside her. The heat that was igniting her blood and making her burn.

And that wasn't the only thing that was burning.

Through the swirling fog of desire and the intoxicating scent of him, came the trace of smoke. Acrid smoke. That unless they'd set fire to the island came from the stove.

With Herculean effort and a rush of alarm, Carla broke away, breathing hard, and put her hands on the rock-solid wall of his chest.

'The garlic,' she managed hoarsely. 'It's burning.'

'*Dio,*' he muttered after a moment in which he looked as dazed as she felt.

Raking his hands through his hair and giving himself a quick shake, Rico stepped back, taking the heat and the madness with him, and went off to investigate the damage, which gave Carla an all too clear view of herself in the mirror that hung over the fireplace. Her hair was a mess, her cheeks bright red and her lips swollen. Her heavy, tingling breasts strained against the bodice of her dress and her legs were spread wide.

Who was this woman in the mirror with the desire-soaked eyes and the heaving chest? Where had that unexpectedly fierce and wanton response come from? She didn't recognise herself. If they hadn't been interrupted she and Rico wouldn't have stopped, and it was suddenly terrifying because this wasn't who she was. She didn't act on instinct and throw caution to the wind with no thought for the consequences. She never allowed herself to be dazzled to distraction by a handsome face and a great body. She took great care to avoid any situation in which the kind of lust that could lay waste to her judgement might arise.

So what had she been thinking? How could she risk destroying the wall around her emotions and the control she'd worked so hard to achieve? Was she insane? More pressingly, how could she and Rico possibly sit down to dinner after *that*? It would be excruciating.

'You know what?' she said, slipping off the island and pulling her dress down with still trembling hands. 'On second thoughts, I'm not really hungry. And I should probably go and make some calls,' she added, unable to look at him as she backed away just as fast as her unsteady legs could carry her. 'So, ah, thanks for your help today and I guess I'll see you in the morning. Goodnight.'

CHAPTER EIGHT

IT WAS GOOD that Carla had fled when she had, Rico thought darkly as he shoved the *linguine alle vongole* he'd finished off making—minus the burnt garlic—into the fridge, his appetite, for food at least, gone. Her sense of self-preservation was clearly as strong as his, even if it had kicked in late.

His, on the other hand, hadn't kicked in at all. He'd taken one look at her, at the challenge and heat in her gaze, and he'd known exactly what she wanted. Too tightly wound and befuddled by need to recall at that precise moment why getting involved with her was a bad idea, he'd succumbed to the temptation to give it to her.

The kiss had been wild and hot, far more explosive than anything he'd imagined. The minute their mouths had met desire had erupted inside him, powering along his veins and channelling all his blood to his groin. The longer the kiss had gone on, the hotter and harder he'd become, and if she hadn't stopped him he'd have leaned her back, pushed her dress up and taken her right there and then. The entire kitchen could have been on fire and he wouldn't have noticed.

What the hell had he been thinking? he wondered, still dazed by the intensity of the encounter, as he switched the lights off and crossed the hall to his flight of stairs with barely a glance in the direction of hers. Where had his control gone? And why on earth had he approached her in the first place? Everything had been fine until he'd stalked round to her side of the island and foolishly positioned himself within reaching distance of her in a move designed to scare her off but which had spectacularly backfired.

Well, maybe not that fine, he mentally amended, striding into his room, tossing the T-shirt she'd pulled off him into the laundry bin and shuddering at the memory of how warm and soft her hands had felt on his naked skin.

Despite his outward cool, he'd been on shaky ground ever since they'd met. On her arrival in Venice cracks had begun to appear when he'd realised how tempting she was but how dangerous she could be. And when she'd stood there in the gym and questioned him about the accident, those cracks had opened up into great, jagged fissures.

He didn't like the burgeoning possibility that his accident could have affected him emotionally as well as physically. The idea that he had some-how been fundamentally altered by what had happened was troubling. Yet, there was no denying that he'd experienced more doubt, bewilderment and wariness in the last three months than he had in the last two decades, and who was he if he wasn't the man who was supremely confident in what he did, who'd always thrived on risk and recklessness and to hell with the consequences?

Nor did he appreciate the stirring up of his past. He hated thinking about the senseless death of his parents at the hand of a recklessly overtaking driver who'd ripped him from everything he'd ever known. Family. Home. Love. And he *never* allowed himself to wonder how his life might have turned out had they lived.

He didn't wish to revisit any of those memories in any great detail, or contemplate his regret at having repeatedly run away from his foster carer in search of what he'd thought would be a better life, with a need to take control. He certainly wasn't ready to welcome back the maelstrom of feelings he'd had at the time, which had become so overwhelming, so unbearable, that he'd shut them down. He doubted he ever would be, and that was all right with him.

What *wasn't* all right was allowing Carla to have pushed that far in the first place. He should have put a stop to it sooner, when he could have done so with a cooler head. Despite having had virtually no experience of that kind of conversation, he should have pressed her for more instead of allowing her to fight back. But even though he hadn't, he should have been one hundred per cent ready for whatever she chose to throw at him.

However, he'd failed at that too.

He didn't know why he'd been so rocked to learn that he'd been born in Argentina and was one of three. As he'd told her, he'd always known he was adopted, so it shouldn't make any difference where he'd been born. Nor should it matter how many siblings he potentially had. He wasn't interested in one, let alone two.

So why did the letter that his parents had left with a law firm in Milan, which he'd been told about at the age of eighteen and ruthlessly ignored, suddenly now seem significant?

On learning of its existence he'd instructed the solicitor to do whatever he liked with it, since its contents held zero appeal. He'd already been on his way to making his first fortune. Every gamble he'd taken had paid off and everything he'd touched had turned to gold. He'd been living the hedonistic life his new-found wealth afforded him and he absolutely had not needed a reminder of his past, of the crucifying rejection and abandonment he'd felt in the aftermath of his parents' death, the gaping hole they'd left, and how vulnerable and gullible he'd once been.

Now, as he unbuckled his belt and shucked off his shorts, he wondered what had become of it. Had the solicitor done as he'd instructed and destroyed it? What had it contained? Could it have held information about the circumstances of his birth? He couldn't seriously be contemplating trying to track it down, could he?

The crushing pressure of now questioning everything he'd always considered a certainty was pushing him to the end of his tether and fraying his control. All day he'd been on edge, and it was largely down to Carla, who he wanted with a fierceness that blew him away. Who dazzled him and robbed him of reason and possibly now knew more about him than he'd realised he'd revealed. Who was just as tenacious and dangerous as he'd suspected and had to be kept at arm's length by whatever means possible.

Tuesday morning, he thought grimly, stepping into the shower and turning it on to cold, couldn't come fast enough.

With her body clock finally back on track Carla should have slept beautifully. She should have woken up firing on all cylinders, feeling strong and invincible and raring to go.

Unfortunately, however, the kiss in the kitchen

the night before had put paid to any rest she'd been hoping for. The heat…the passion…the wanton yet terrifying lack of control… If she hadn't been jolted back to reality by the burning garlic she and Rico would have had hot, wild sex right then and there, and that was something she just couldn't seem to stop imagining.

The sizzling memory of it and the myriad questions she had about the scars on his chest, not to mention the intense emotion that had blazed in his eyes, which she'd never seen before in him but which confirmed her suspicion that still waters ran deep, had kept her tossing and turning in bed for hours. Exhaustion had finally won out in the early hours, and as a result she woke up feeling gritty and on edge, her nerves frayed by desire she just couldn't shake no matter how hard she tried.

And now they were going to be spending most of the day together.

Petrified of bumping into Rico over breakfast and having to make horrendously awkward chat, Carla waited for the all clear before darting into the kitchen and grabbing a pastry from the fridge while keeping her gaze firmly away from the scene of the crime.

On the dot of eight she arrived at the helipad that was situated a couple of hundred metres from the house. Rico was already there, mirrored sunglasses concealing his eyes, his expression unreadable, the headset he had on thankfully precluding conversation.

Apparently as disinclined to acknowledge what had happened last night as she was, he barely glanced at her as she climbed aboard. He merely handed her a headset of her own and coolly indicated that she should buckle herself in before returning his attention to the dozens of dials and switches in front of him.

Moments later, the engine fired and the rotors started turning, and then they were up and away, soaring above the lagoon, leaving Isola Santa Margherita far behind and heading for the mainland, hurtling through the air in such a tiny contraption at such a great speed that her stomach was in her throat, while she clung on to her seat, her knuckles white.

To her relief, Rico's concentration on what he was doing, combined with the noise of the helicopter, prevented any further communication. But as the journey continued, the urban sprawl giving way to a patchwork of fields dotted with villages, Lake Garda in the distance and the foothills of the Italian Alps beyond, and her nerves began to ease, she became increasingly aware of him.

The space was naturally confined and he filled it. His masculine scent surrounded her, making her head swim and her mouth water. Every inch of him was within touching distance. His thigh was unsettlingly close to hers. If she moved even a millimetre to the left, her shoulder would brush against his. Focusing on *not* doing that, when they kept being buffeted about by the wind, was taking every drop of strength she possessed, as was keeping her eyes off him.

It was so hard not to stare at his profile and linger on the scar and the slight bump in his nose which gave him the hint of badness that she found so attractive. So hard not to look at his fingers wrapped around the stick that he was using to fly this thing and not remember them in her hair and on her skin. She'd always had a penchant for competence, and it was even harder not to melt into a puddle of lust at just how skilled he was at the controls.

But not impossible.

Because of far greater importance than any of that was the clock counting down her time in Italy, which was ticking louder and louder with every passing second. Patience while waiting for seeds of suggestion to take root was all very well but in this situation she needed to get a move on.

Last night's attempts to lull Rico into a false sense of security hadn't exactly worked, so quid pro quo was how she was going to proceed, she decided, blocking out the infuriatingly unsettling effect his proximity was having on her and focusing. A back and forth of information that she'd start and force him to follow.

This time, *she* was going to control the conversation and she might have to dig deeper than she'd have ideally liked, but by carefully revealing to him layers of herself no one else apart from Georgie had ever seen she'd show him he had nothing to fear. She certainly didn't. She had no doubt that Rico wouldn't respond in an emotional sense to whatever she told him. Her revelations would bounce right off the steel-plated armour he surrounded himself with. He didn't let anyone close and she saw no reason he'd ever decide to make an exception for her. Apart from the sensational chemistry they shared, which this morning he was ignoring in the same way she was trying to but with a greater degree of success, he simply didn't have a sufficient level of interest to bother. Or any, in fact. Which was totally fine with her.

There was no point in waiting until another monosyllabic meal, she told herself, mentally unlocking the past and bracing herself for the reality of laying it out in front of this man. If she really was going to do this—and for the sake of her best friend she absolutely was—she had to strike while the iron was hot. And that meant implementing her plan as soon as they landed.

* * *

Generally Rico got a massive kick out of flying his helicopter, but as he landed the machine at Linate Airport and switched off the engine he thought he'd never been so glad to see the back of it.

The trip to Milan had been nothing short of torture. He'd been agonisingly aware of Carla sitting beside him, close enough to touch, close enough to pull onto his lap and kiss the living daylights out of again, so damn affecting that he might as well not have bothered with the numerous cold showers he'd taken throughout the very long night.

The tension in his muscles was excruciating. His jaw was so tight it was on the point of shattering. The restraint he was having to exercise, a novel concept he had no intention of repeating ever again once she'd gone, was intolerable.

Why was it so hard to control his response to her? he wondered darkly as he jumped down and then strode around the front to help her alight too. Was this yet another effect of his accident? Another weakening of the defences he'd always considered impregnable?

Whatever it was, he didn't like it, any more than he liked the strength of his desire for her. He'd experienced need before, many times, but the intensity and the wildness with which he wanted *her* was new. What was it about her that was different? Why did she and she alone affect him in this way?

Releasing her hand as soon as she was on solid ground as if it were on fire, Rico turned on his heel and made for the car that was waiting for them on the tarmac. With a nod to Marco, his chauffeur in Milan, who was opening the door for Carla, he climbed in and slammed the door shut. Once she was in too it hit him that, since the car was as spacious as the helicopter, the journey to the consulate was going to be equally torturous. Possibly even more so, since now he didn't have the distraction of flying, which was why he *had* to stop thinking about both the incredibly passionate way she'd responded to him last night and the astonishingly good feel of her beneath his hands.

'So,' she said, making herself comfortable before taking off her sunglasses and turning to face him, something about the set of her jaw and the determined look in her eye raising the hairs on the back of his neck. 'Milan.'

'What about it?' he said, aiming for the cool nonchalance that so often eluded him when she was in his vicinity, and, for once, just about nailing it.

'It's where you started on your journey to fund management world domination.'

'I wouldn't put it quite like that.'

'Then how would you put it?' she asked. 'The article I read described you as mysteriously elusive, but a man with the Midas touch, which I guess would explain the island, the private jet and the helicopter.'

'The jet and the helicopter do save time,' he said, reflecting that the description of him was apt, although none of his success had been by design. He'd had no ambition to make a fortune when he'd been given a chance to escape a life of crime and despair. He'd had no plans at all and nothing to lose, so he'd taken risks with little care for the consequences. In a fairer world he'd have squandered everything several times over, but his world had had other ideas and rewarded every reckless move he'd made, as if making amends for everything he'd once had and lost.

'And what do you do with the time you save?'

'I manage to keep myself entertained.'

'I'm sure you do,' she said smoothly. 'So tell me what led you into it.'

Not a chance. 'Only if you tell me first what took you into crisis management,' he countered with a wide, easy grin, confident that she'd back right off since when it came to personal information she dodged and feinted as much as he did.

'All right.'

What? As the word exploded between them

like some kind of bomb, every cell of his body froze and his stomach roiled. Damn. 'I was joking.'

'I wasn't,' she said calmly and he realised with a stab of alarm and a jolt of panic that she really wasn't. 'And I'm going to hold you to it.'

'No need.'

'There's every need.'

'Why don't you tell me about your favourite band instead?' he said, never more regretting the fact that they were speeding along a motorway and therefore unable to screech to a stop so he could get the hell out.

'The main reason I went into crisis management,' she said, clearly deciding to give that absurd question the consideration it deserved, which was none, 'was to put something bad that happened to me to good use.'

At that, Rico snapped his head round and went very still, his heart giving a great thud. And even though the very *last* thing he wanted to be having was this conversation, even though he knew he ought to respond with something flippant designed to shut her down and maintain the distance, instead he found himself saying, 'Something bad?'

'When I was fifteen, I was groomed.'

What the hell? What did that even mean? 'What happened?'

'As I told you, my parents are hippies and I was raised on various communes. They were too busy smoking weed and chanting to pay me any attention, so I went in search of it myself. One afternoon I was hanging out in an internet cafe and I got chatting online to someone I thought was a boy my age.'

'But he wasn't,' he said as sickening realisation began to dawn.

'No,' she said with a slow shake of her head. 'He very definitely wasn't. But he was clever and patient. He asked me all about myself and I told him everything. He took the ammunition I gave him and used it on me quite calculatingly. He knew exactly which buttons to push and how to shower me with the affection and love I craved so desperately. And he knew that when he withdrew it I'd beg him to give it back, which I did.'

Bastardo.

'Within weeks I was addicted to his messages and started skipping school early to get to the cafe. He sent me a phone so we could actually talk and I used it to send him the photos he asked for. When he came clean and told me he was thirty to my fifteen I didn't care. I was in far too deep by that point. It was our secret and it was thrilling and I was obsessed. Before long I stopped hanging out with my friends or talking to anyone but him, really. Georgie tried, but he gave me some great excuses to use and my parents weren't paying any attention to what was going on anyway. When he suggested we meet, I didn't hesitate for a single second. I packed a bag, took the money he'd also sent me and was off.'

'Where did you go?' he asked, his head spinning so fast he was barely able to comprehend what she was telling him.

'I met him in a hotel in east London.'

'Separate rooms?'

'One room. Double bed.'

His jaw clenched so hard it was on the point of shattering. 'And you were fifteen.'

'Yes.'

And he thought he knew the depths of depravity people could sink to. He'd been wrong.

'We spent three days there,' she continued, clearly oblivious to the rage beginning to crash though him. 'The plan was to run away to France but I didn't have a passport, so it was then Scotland, but before that could happen the police turned up.'

'How did they find you?'

'I couldn't resist sending Georgie a photo of the hotel, even though by that point I wasn't letting her speak to me. I thought I was so grown up,' she said with a tiny frown, as if she thought she was somehow to blame, which was staggeringly wrong. 'I was showing off. She called the police. I owe her big time. I still can't believe she didn't cut me off completely. I was vile.'

'It wasn't your fault.'

'No, I know that,' she said that with a nod that, thank God, suggested she not only knew it but also believed it. 'None of it was my fault. It was all *his*.'

'What happened to him?'

'He went to jail, came out, did it again, and went back. As far as I know he's still inside.'

'He'd better stay there,' he muttered, thinking it was for his safety because if he ever got his hands on the *figlio di puttana* he wouldn't be responsible for the outcome.

'He will. For a while, at least,' she said, frowning faintly before rallying. 'So, back to the original question, that's why I went into crisis management. I know how powerful manipulation can be. I know its effects and the way in which it can be used to change people's behaviours and make them believe whatever you want them to believe. It felt like a good fit. I realise it might sound strange, but channelling what happened to me into a successful career has been cathartic. So there we go,' she finished with a quick smile that frankly defied belief. 'That's me. It's your turn now.'

She sat back, regarding him expectantly, while inside he reeled. His turn? He could barely think straight. How could she be so composed when he wanted to hit something for the first time in years?

And how the hell could he not reciprocate after all that? How could he not answer her questions when she'd answered his with such frankness and honesty? He didn't want to simply brush aside what she'd told him, as if it meant nothing. It didn't. Not to her.

He'd never told a living soul what he'd been through, but how much of a risk would it really be to share with her some of it the way she had with him? In one sense at least, her experiences hadn't been all that dissimilar to his. They'd both been used, manipulated and exploited for the benefit of others. She had to know some of the disillusionment he'd once felt, the shattering of hopes and dreams and the determination to never allow it to happen again. Any revelation he chose to make would therefore be safe with her. He had nothing to fear. He hoped.

'What do you want to know?' he said, and the look of relief that filled her expression, as if she'd fully expected him to refuse to stick to his side of the bargain despite everything she'd told him, was like a blow to the gut. He might have many flaws, but a lack of integrity wasn't one of them nowadays.

'What made you go into fund management?'

'I was given an opportunity and took it,' he said, silently vowing to at least try to be as open and honest as she'd been in an effort not to disappoint her.

'When?'

'When I was sixteen.'

Her eyebrows lifted. 'That's young.'

To some, perhaps. But not to him. He'd lived two brutal lifetimes by that age. 'I started off at an investment bank working as a clerk. In a year I'd acquired the qualifications necessary to trade on La Borsa.'

'The Italian stock exchange?'

'*Corretto*. It's here in Milan. I told you I was good with numbers. Well, I was also good at spotting opportunities no one else could see. I took risks and they paid off. I made my first million at eighteen. When I was twenty-four, I left to set up my own fund. I had no trouble picking up clients. I now have six billion euros under management.'

'All on your own?'

'With the exception of some back office support, yes.'

'That's quite an achievement.'

'As is yours.'

'We're not quite in the same league,' she said with a wry grin—a real one—that lit her eyes and stole his breath, before it disappointingly disappeared and her expression sobered. 'So where were you for the six years between your parents' death and starting work at this investment bank?'

He tensed, every fibre of his being demanding that he shut up, but he wasn't going to. He'd agreed to this and he didn't go back on his word these days, no matter how great the temptation. 'Initially I went into foster care,' he said, forcing himself to relax while telling himself it would be fine.

'You had no other relatives?'

If only. 'No. I lived with four different families in two years. Every time I thought I was settled I got moved on like an unwanted parcel. Eventually I decided that *I'd* be in charge of where I lived. I ran away. Frequently. At first I was caught and returned, but after a while they simply stopped looking.'

She stared at him, her eyes wide and filling with an emotion he couldn't begin to identify. 'Just like that?'

'Pretty much. I was very good at hiding.'

'What did you do?'

'I lived on the streets for a while, sleeping in doorways by night and scavenging for food by day. But then it started getting colder. One night I broke into an empty building, only to discover that it wasn't an empty building. It turned out to be the headquarters of I Picaresqui, which was then one of the most notorious street gangs in

Veneto. They thought I might be a spy for the police.'

'Oh, my God. What happened?'

'You saw the scars,' he said, remembering the way the fire had scorched his skin, the panic and the terror that had scythed through him.

A flush bloomed on her cheeks for a moment. 'The two on your upper chest looked like cigarette burns,' she said, her voice strangely husky and tight.

'They are.'

'And the others?' she asked, her gaze lifting to the scar at his temple and the bump in his nose.

'A fight with a rival gang member over territory a year or two later.'

Her eyes jerked back to his, the shock he saw in them sending a dart of what felt like shame shooting through him. 'You *joined* them?'

'*Si,*' he said, stamping it out since he didn't need judgement. From anyone, least of all her. He'd judged himself plenty.

'Why?'

'It felt like a good idea at the time.'

'What sort of things did you have to do?'

'I started off by fleecing unsuspecting tourists,' he said, sticking to the facts and the facts alone. 'Pickpocketing and coin tricks were my speciality, but anything really that made money quickly. You asked me why my English was so good.'

'I remember.'

'It *is* the language of business and I *do* have an ear for it, but I also spent a lot of time watching films and reading books in order to be able to scam tourists better.'

'I bet you were good at it.'

'I was. Very.'

'And then?'

'Once I'd earned the respect of the leaders, I moved into the accounting side of the business.'

There was no need to tell her some of the other more brutal things, more shameful things he'd had to do to prove himself loyal—the fighting, the righting of perceived wrongs, the collecting of debts. Or about the complex tangle of feelings he'd once had about it all.

'Did you ever get caught?'

'I spent more nights in the cells than I care to remember.'

'No wonder you have a thing about police stations,' she said, which proved once again how sharp she was. 'You were tense,' she said in response to the quizzical look he gave her. 'I noticed.'

'You fainted.'

'It brought back painful memories for me too,' she said, her eyes clouding for a moment, and he had to fight back an urge to demand more. He didn't need more. He'd never need more.

'So how did you get out?' she asked, yanking his thoughts back on track. 'How on earth did you go from being part of a gang to working at an investment bank in Milan?'

'I was arrested on money-laundering charges and hauled in front of a judge. I confessed to nothing, but during the course of the trial my skill with money and numbers kept cropping up. It was never clear quite what the judge saw in me, but one morning she told me she had a contact here and gave me a choice. Jail or a job. I chose the latter and now I exploit the markets, which when I think about it is as ironic as you manipulating perception for your job. What?' he finished with a frown, not liking the strange look that was appearing on her face one little bit.

'We're kindred spirits,' she said with a softness that he hoped to God wasn't pity. 'Who knew?'

'We're nothing of the kind,' he muttered with a sharp shudder as he glanced at the building in front of which they were pulling up and thought he'd never been so grateful to arrive at a destination. 'What we *are*, is here.'

CHAPTER NINE

THE BUSINESS OF procuring her new passport prevented any further conversation beyond the practical, but that didn't stop Carla's head spinning with everything that Rico had told her in the car.

When she'd finished telling her tale, which oddly hadn't been as difficult as she'd feared, and prompted him to reveal his, she'd never *dreamt* it could be as upsetting as it had been.

The things he'd been through... The loss of his parents... The shunting between foster families and finding himself on the streets... And then the horrors of the gang he'd joined that she couldn't even *begin* to imagine...

He'd been so young. He'd suffered so much. He'd been abandoned and then left to fend for himself. He'd been tortured, by the sounds of things, and she was sure that wasn't all of it. How could her heart not have twisted and ached for him? How could she not have burned up with the injustice of it? She could barely bring herself to think about the brutality he must have experienced. And yet he'd been so cool, so unfazed as he'd recounted the desperate nature of his childhood, as if he were talking about someone else entirely.

How had he achieved that level of acceptance? she wondered, her eyes still stinging faintly and her throat still tight as they were ushered into an office without Rico even having to give his name. Had shutting himself down been the only way to handle the impact of his experiences? Was that why he'd chosen to cut himself off from others both geographically and emotionally?

It was astonishing he was as together as he was, in all honesty. Unlike her, it didn't sound as if he'd had any support, at least in the emotional sense. Unlike her, he'd had to make sense of everything entirely on his own. Yet, somehow, *like* her, he'd come through it and used it to make a success of his life. His determination and resilience matched her own. As did the lengths he went to in order to protect himself.

So where else might the similarities lie? she couldn't help wondering, even though it had no bearing on anything. They'd both lacked a proper home with roots. They both had an insanely strong work ethic and a reluctance to share personal information. Apart from unbelievable chemistry, what else might they have in common?

She didn't get the opportunity to probe further and find out. The consul himself—whose wife apparently ran a charity supporting homeless kids, which Rico generously supported, hence the owed favour—appeared within moments and ten minutes later, having obtained her passport, she and Rico were heading for the exit.

But when she suggested taking a tour of the city with the aim of continuing their earlier conversation under the guise of seeing the sights, he claimed he needed to get back to work. Her subsequent invitation to lunch was refused, and when she told him she knew how he felt about skipping meals he merely muttered something about grabbing a sandwich at the airport.

The guard he'd momentarily dropped for her had shot back up, she realised in the car on the way back to his helicopter—a journey spent in an uncomfortably prickly silence—and it was more disappointing than she could have imagined, because she sensed there was so much more to him and his story.

Never mind the fact that she'd revealed nothing of the effects her experience had had on her. She wanted to know more about how *his* had affected *him*. Not for Finn, who'd be fine with the facts, but for herself. Now she'd had a glimpse of the intriguing man beneath the surface, she wanted to smash through his defences and find out everything.

And not just on that front.

His continued indifference to her after what had happened last night was another source of increasing bewilderment and distress, even though she really ought not to be thinking about it at all. Why wasn't he suffering from her proximity the way she was from his? was the shameful thought that kept running through her head. Why, when he'd mentioned the occasion she'd seen the scars on his chest, had he remained so unmoved, while she'd instantly caught fire? How could he continue to act as if nothing had happened?

Maybe he really had wiped it from his mind. Perhaps what she'd assumed to be denial was, in actual fact, a complete lack of interest. Perhaps she'd in some way disappointed him. And yet she hadn't imagined the heat and fierceness of their kiss, or his loss of control that had gone with it. The swirling intensity of his eyes, blazing into hers, was seared onto her memory.

And she might as well admit she wanted more of it all.

In the absence of conversation, the desire she'd managed to get under some sort of control while they'd been talking was flooding back, drumming through her with increasing potency with every passing moment, and by the time they

were back in the helicopter and once again flying over the land below she couldn't help feeling
that perhaps she'd been a bit pathetic by fleeing
his kitchen like that.

Since when did she run away from anything
these days? Why hadn't she stayed and handled
the hot situation with the cool she was capable
of? She'd dealt with far worse. So what had she
been so afraid of? How awful would it have been
if she hadn't been distracted by the burning garlic
and things had reached their natural conclusion?

She had nothing to fear from Rico or the fierce
passion he aroused in her. They weren't *really*
kindred spirits, despite her overly dramatic proc-
lamation, which had been made in a rare moment
of emotional weakness, and it wasn't as if she
was actually contemplating a relationship with
the man. The last thing she wanted was commitment, or any kind of emotional intimacy, for that
matter, when emotions involving the opposite sex
were so dangerous, but he clearly wasn't all that
keen on attachment either.

So surely there was nothing stopping her having one night with him, she told herself, going a
bit giddy at the very thought of it. She was leaving in the morning. She could embrace and ex-
plore the desire she felt for him without the fear of
being manipulated or sucked in any deeper, and

she could depart with no looking back and no regrets. Who knew when she'd next get the chance?

She wanted him, quite desperately, and, while whether he still wanted her was another matter, one thing was certain—she would never know if she didn't ask.

Now they were back, Rico needed to remove himself from Carla's vicinity before he made a move from which there would be no return.

Two moves, actually.

First off, it appeared that revealing the barest details of his life to date had acted as something of a trigger and he'd found himself wanting to tell her not only everything but also how he felt about it all, which was wholly unacceptable and made absolutely no sense.

Why would he *ever* want to do that? he'd asked himself while she'd been signing the forms and taking possession of the travel document that was so important to her. To create that kind of connection he'd have to be mad, and even he couldn't be so reckless as to risk that kind of insanity.

Nevertheless, despite his best efforts to put it from his mind he'd been so unsettled by their conversation in the car he'd automatically answered her question about the favour owed him by the consul, and at that point he'd realised he'd be better off not talking at all.

Which brought him to move number two, namely the increasingly difficult to resist desire hammering away inside him that in the absence of conversation had swollen to unbearable proportions.

He hated the fact that it was so hard to control. He couldn't shake the disturbing feeling that one tiny loosening of his grip on it would unravel him completely. He didn't want to want Carla—she'd been bang on about that—any more than he wanted to keep dwelling on what she'd told him about being so sickeningly abused. He didn't want to wonder how she'd felt about it then or how she felt about it now, or what long-lasting effects it might have had. He wasn't jealous of the support she'd had in the shape of a best friend. The stab of shame that he'd felt when he'd caught the appalled shock in her eyes at his confession he'd actually joined the gang, as if he'd somehow let her down, had been wholly unnecessary. He had no need to apologise for anything. There was no point in regretting anything he'd done and it didn't matter one jot if he disappointed her. Why did he care about proving to her his integrity? They weren't kindred spirits. They couldn't be.

The crushing pressure of everything battering at his head and body was too much to bear and he didn't know how much longer he'd be able to hold it together. So he was going to hole up in his study until six o'clock in the morning, repairing the dent in his fortune and those of his clients while cobbling together some sort of control over everything he was suffering, and to hell with whether that made him a lily-livered coward and a terrible host. Carla could fend for herself. He'd had enough.

'Rico, wait.'

Nope. Not happening. She was probably going to thank him and he didn't think he could take her gratitude when he wanted something else entirely from her yet shouldn't and couldn't have. But apparently she was not to be deterred because his progress back to the house wasn't as fast as he'd have liked it to be and within seconds she'd caught up with him.

'Stop,' she said, panting slightly in a distracting way and planting a hand on his bare forearm, which singed his skin and rooted him to the spot.

'What is it?' he snapped, too frayed to even attempt to make a stab at cool, easy-going levity.

'I have a question. About last night.'

That was worse than any thank-you. 'There's nothing to discuss,' he muttered, shaking her off and resuming his march to the house.

'I think there is.'

'In what way?'

'What would have happened if the garlic hadn't burned?'

What the hell? 'What do you think would have happened?' he said, the memories of their kiss burning through him and having their inevitable effect.

'I think we wouldn't have stopped. I think we'd have had sex right there on your kitchen island.'

His pulse began to gallop, the images smashing into his head, desire breaking through the flimsy dam he'd constructed and coursing through him in a great rush of molten heat. He wanted to deny it, but it was impossible. 'Well, then. There you go. Is that it?'

'I hope not.'

His brows snapped together and he wheeled round to face her. 'What do you mean by that?'

She took a deep breath and looked him square in the eye. 'I want to finish what we started.'

He tensed, fighting with every inch of his control the clamouring urge to grab hold of her and do exactly that. 'That is not a good idea.'

'Why not?'

Yes, quite. Why not? 'It's complicated,' he muttered, shoving his hands in the pockets of his shorts, any pretence of equanimity long gone.

'It needn't be.'

Nevertheless, it was. For a whole host of reasons. He didn't know who he was these days. He understood none of the things he'd done recently. And then there was his unwise interest in the woman standing in front of him and his curiosity about all the things they had in common and those they very much did not. His heart banged against his ribcage while his head throbbed with the intensity of the pressure pushing in on him from all sides. 'I'm injured.'

'I'd take care.'

But what if he didn't? What if he let his guard down even more than he already had? What if she somehow tripped him up and before he knew it had him telling her everything? Or worse, wound up wanting more than he could ever give?

'It would just be one afternoon and one night, Rico,' she said, as if able to read his mind. 'My flight is booked for the morning and that's not going to change. There's no room in my life for a relationship. Seriously. You'd be perfectly safe from me.'

Safe? Really? He'd never met anyone quite so threatening.

But, *Dio*, her words rang in his ears like a siren call, tempting him across the calm waters of reason towards the treacherous rocks of hedonistic ecstasy.

One afternoon. One night. Free of strings. Free of complications. Drenched in pleasure. He hadn't felt this alert, this alive in months. And as for his ability to perform... Pain? What pain? The only ache he had right now was deep in his pelvis. He wanted her as badly as she'd just admitted she wanted him, and really, would it be so bad? How dangerous could she possibly be? He'd never allowed a woman to expect more than what he was able to offer and he wasn't about to start now. And wouldn't actually acting on the desire make it lessen, or even obliterate it altogether?

As the reasons for objecting ran out and the last of his resistance crumbled, Rico reached for her, pulled her against him and slammed his mouth down on hers.

Oh, thank God for that.

For the longest of moments, Carla had really thought Rico was going to stick to his guns in refusing her request and she'd been all ready to back down, since a no was, after all, a no, even a humiliating one. But to her relief he'd obviously had a change of heart because the next thing she knew she was in his arms and he was kissing her as if his life depended on it.

She softened and melted into him instantly, parting her lips and moaning his name as they came together in a clash of teeth and tongues and a tangle of hands. She wound her arms around his neck and pressed herself close, and at the feel of him, so big and solid against her, shivers shot down her spine.

To actually be able to touch him after a morning spent resisting the urge to do exactly that was utterly intoxicating and she couldn't get enough. She ran her hands over his shoulders and down his arms and he shuddered and groaned into her mouth. His muscles tensed with every caress and she could feel his granite-hard erection pressed against her.

With one hand he angled her head and deepened the kiss, and her breasts tightened and tingled, her nipples stiffening with the need to be touched. With the other he pulled her hips more tightly to him, sending shocks of electricity spiralling through her.

When he pulled back, breathing raggedly, he looked as if he was in as much of a fog as she was. The blue of his eyes had darkened to the deepest navy, the desperate hunger she could see in them reflecting the frantic need she knew her own contained. Before he could have time to even *think* about the wisdom of what he was doing she breathed huskily, 'Complete the tour and show me your room,' and thankfully he didn't need to be told twice.

Taking her hand, he strode into the house and across the hall. At the bottom of his stairs he stopped, his eyes blazing and a muscle pounding in his jaw, and said, 'Go on ahead.' In response to the quizzical look she gave him, he merely added,

'I had a fantasy about exactly this scenario only yesterday afternoon.'

'What was I doing?' she said, her pulse thudding heavily at the dizzying realisation that he'd imagined this, just as she had.

'Simply walking up the stairs.'

'I think I can do better than that.'

She turned and began slowly climbing the stairs, swinging her hips and running her fingers over the banister as she went. Halfway up, she paused to look over her shoulder and give him a wicked grin, and the intensity with which he was watching her knocked the breath from her lungs. At the top, she crooked her finger at him, and within seconds he'd taken the steps two at a time.

'How was that?' she breathed as he led her into his bedroom with indecent haste.

'Better than I could possibly have imagined.'

He had her back in his arms in a flash and in between hot, frantic kisses she tugged on his T-shirt while he shoved her top up, only releasing her so that they could free themselves of items that neither had any need for. Jeans and shorts and shoes immediately followed and then he was backing her towards the bed and tumbling her onto the mattress.

For a moment, as she lay sprawled on the sheets catching her breath, he just stood there staring at her as if he'd never seen a nearly naked woman before, and while every cell of her body quivered in response to the heat of his gaze she took the opportunity to do the same.

Everywhere she looked she saw hard muscle and tanned skin, his broad chest and powerful thighs sprinkled with a smattering of rough, dark hair. In the region of his hips and pelvis were scars which, in contrast to those on his chest, were livid and recent, presumably a result of the surgery he'd had to have. But she couldn't have asked him about them even if she'd wanted to. All her attention was drawn to the enormous erection that lay beneath the fabric of his black shorts and made her pulse race and her mouth water.

As stunning as the view was, though, the desperation throbbing inside her was becoming intolerable.

'What are you waiting for?' she said with a seductiveness that was surprising even to her ears.

'You're too perfect.'

If only he knew, she thought, the gruffness of his voice tugging at something deep inside her. She might not have too many lumps and bumps on the outside, but the fears and doubts she had on the inside more than made up for it. 'Believe me, I am far from perfect. But I am burning up with desire for you. I need you. Now, Rico.'

He must have heard the desperation in her voice because in an instant he'd joined her on the bed. He lowered himself on top of her, pressing her down with his delicious weight, his hardness a heady contrast to her softness. With a rough groan he brought his head down to hers and captured her mouth with a mind-blowing kiss, and she wound her legs around his hips and her arms around his neck until she was enveloped by his scent and warmth and her head cleared of everything but him.

After a moment that seemed to stretch for hours he rolled onto his back, taking her with him, which had her straddling him and rubbing herself against his erection, her breaths coming in short, ragged pants while he undid the clasp of her bra. She shrugged it off, her blood thick and hot, her pulse thundering, and a moment later he flipped her back over.

'Nifty,' she gasped.

'A miracle, quite frankly,' he murmured. 'A couple of days ago a move like that would have had me reaching for the painkillers.'

She grinned and then he cupped her breast, his palm fitting to her perfectly, and her smile gave way to a sigh as sensation skated through her body. She arched her back and he trailed kisses down her throat, across the slope of her chest and took her hard nipple in his mouth. She moaned his name and grabbed his hair, and when he moved his other hand down her body, his fingers slipping beneath the waistband of her knickers and then into her tight, slick heat, she gasped.

He transferred his attention to her other breast while he rubbed her clitoris with his thumb, his fingers moving inside her, and all coherent thought fled. When he shifted and moved and added to her torment by putting his mouth to the spot where his fingers and thumb were creating such devastation she nearly leapt off the bed.

'Enough,' she panted after a few minutes of agonisingly exquisite torment.

'No.'

'Yes. I want you inside me when I come. Don't make me beg.'

'It has a certain appeal.'

'Don't.'

He gave her a hot, hard kiss, which dazzled her senses, and then he reared up, reached over and rummaged around in the drawer of his nightstand. Ogling his back, she heard the crinkle of a foil packet, the harsh hiss of breath, and then he came back to her, sliding her knickers down and off. She opened her legs wide and he settled between them, and as he crushed his mouth to hers he thrust into her with one long, hard stroke and the pleasure was so exquisite she nearly came right there and then.

Lodged deep inside her, he stilled, but she

didn't need time to adjust to him so she dug her fingers into the taut muscles of his buttocks to pull him in further and gave her hips a quick twist, which seemed to do the trick.

With a harsh groan he pulled out of her and then back in, and did it again and again, setting a rhythm that started off slow, drugging her with desire, but became harder and faster within seconds until her breath was coming in increasingly short, sharp pants. Her entire body was on fire and she could feel the tension coiling deep inside her, swelling and tightening, and just when she thought she couldn't stand it any longer he kissed her hard, and suddenly she was flying apart, ecstasy exploding inside her like fireworks. With a great rough groan Rico thrust into her one last time, as deep as he could, and exploded, pulsating into her over and over again.

'I thought you were supposed to be injured,' she said once she'd regained enough breath to speak.

'I believe I've made a miraculous recovery,' he said, sounding as dazed as she was.

'So it would seem,' she said, feeling him twitch and harden inside her. 'Which is a shame.'

'Is it?' he murmured, one dark eyebrow raised. 'Why?'

'I was going to offer to kiss you better.'

'Well, you know, I'm not *completely* healed,' he said with a slow, devastating smile.

'Where do you hurt?'

'Everywhere.'

CHAPTER TEN

THE ALARM THAT went off on the phone Rico had
lent to Carla shattered the early-morning peace
and jolted him out of the deepest sleep he'd had
in years, which on the one hand was surprising
when he usually slept fitfully, but on the other
wasn't, given that night had been making way for
dawn by the time they had finally crashed out.

He'd never had a night like it, he thought, giving his eyes a quick rub and his body a stretch
that made his muscles twinge. He didn't think
he'd ever forget the sight of Carla sidling up his
stairs—his fantasy brought to life, only better—
and then lying sprawled on his bed, a goddess of
his very own in all her nearly naked perfection.
Nor would he ever forget the scent and taste of
her, spicy and sweet, or the wildness of her response.

For the briefest of moments it had struck him
that he shouldn't be sullying her perfection with
all his flaws and the murky history of the things

he'd done, but then she'd revealed how much she'd wanted him and his mind had gone blank. The minute he'd put his hands and mouth on her that had been that for rational thought. He'd been swamped with heat and desire and sensation and had had no sense of time.

Eventually, driven by hunger of an entirely different kind, he'd brought up the linguine from the night before, which they'd devoured before going for a late-night dip in the pool that had been less of a swim than a hot, wet tangle of limbs that had resulted in a lot of water being sloshed over the side.

He'd lost count of the number of orgasms he'd given and received. Even though he said it himself, for someone who'd recently had the kind of accident that required surgery and rehabilitation, his stamina had been impressive. But then, he'd had a powerful incentive. He'd forgotten how much he enjoyed the sharp sensations that came with sex and the sweet oblivion that followed. How intensely he felt, how sensationally he came alive.

Not that he'd ever had sex like this. He'd never met anyone like Carla, who so easily matched his voracious demands and wasn't afraid to make some of her own. He'd never experienced pleasure so great it blew the top of his head off.

It was a shame she was leaving. He wouldn't

mind some more, because instead of going away, as he'd idiotically assumed it would, his need for her had only got stronger. But she *was* leaving. And that was that.

Unless it wasn't…

Maybe she didn't have to go just yet, he thought, his pulse suddenly pounding, every muscle in his body tensing at the realisation that perhaps he could have more. Maybe she could stick around for a little while longer. Hadn't she told him she'd arranged a week's leave? Hadn't she said she had no real plans? What if he asked her to stay? Not for ever, never that, but certainly until she had to return home to work.

If she said no, that would be that. After her revelations about her youth, there was no way in hell he'd try and manipulate her into changing her mind. He'd accept her decision with good grace, see her off and set about restarting his interrupted plan to get back to the life he'd had prior to his accident.

But he badly hoped she'd say yes, because he wasn't ready to let her go.

With the echo of the alarm still ringing in her ears, Carla shifted and yawned, achingly aware of the devastatingly talented man lying beside her, who'd taken her to heaven and back several times over the course of yesterday afternoon and last night. She opened her eyes to find him propped up on an elbow, watching her with an expression that was as unfathomable as it was intense, and gave him an unstoppable smile.

'*Buon giorno,*' he said, his sleep-roughened voice sending shivers rippling through her and bringing with it a hot flurry of scorchingly vivid memories of everything they'd done together.

'I don't know about that,' she murmured, feeling herself flush and stamping down hard on the regret that they wouldn't be doing any of it again. 'It's horrendously early. But I should start packing. My flight leaves in less than two hours.'

'Stay.'

At the huskily uttered word—not quite a suggestion, not quite a demand—Carla went very still. 'What?'

'Stay.'

Was he joking? He didn't look as if he was. He looked more serious than she'd ever seen him. So could she be dreaming? Nope. She was awake. *Wide* awake now.

What was he doing?

Perhaps the novelty of sex after three long months without it—to which he'd confessed while heating up the linguine—had addled his brain. Or perhaps it was the lack of sleep. He'd gone out like a light the minute his head hit the pillows he'd retrieved off the floor after they'd taken a long, hot shower to wash the chlorine from the pool off each other. She'd taken a while longer, partly because he'd spread himself across the vast bed as if trying to occupy as much space as possible, which had left her perilously close to the edge, and partly because he was not a peaceful sleeper. He twitched and shifted as if the slightest noise might have him sitting bolt upright—a hang-up from his life on the streets?—and it had made her conscious of her breathing, which had kept her awake for a while.

'I thought we agreed this was a one-night thing only,' she said carefully, willing her strangely galloping pulse to slow down.

'I've changed my mind.'

'Why?'

'You're on leave and I want more.'

Well, so did she, if she was being honest, because she'd never experienced the fiery passion he aroused in her, but extending her stay was out of the question. She had things to do back home. She wasn't sure quite what yet, but the minute she landed she'd be compiling an extensive to-do list.

And despite the head-wrecking pleasure she'd experienced recently she hadn't forgotten the whole justification for deciding to sleep with him in the first place. She needed to leave to protect herself. Rico was far too compelling and fascinating and she couldn't risk developing an interest in him that went beyond the physical. If that happened she'd slide into seriously dangerous territory where her emotions became involved and the very essence of who she was would be at risk.

On the other hand, where was she ever going to get sex like this again? She might as well admit that she was already addicted to the way he made her feel. By sticking to the plan and waltzing off with a breezy smile and a casual wave, might she not be cutting her nose off to spite her face?

She had no doubt that it would be far safer to walk away and continue to live her perfectly fine life, which had no soaring highs but no plummeting lows either, but was that really how she saw the rest of her existence? Didn't that somehow smack of opting out? Didn't it imply that she was still affected by what had happened to her when she was young?

What if she actually took a risk for a change? So what if they talked? Where was the danger in that? She was struggling to continue to deny the curiosity burning up inside her. She was desperate to get to know the man beneath the surface, and it wasn't as if she was going to lose control or anything. While Rico's interest in her was flattering, it was hardly something she would let go to her head, and with his detachment she had no need to worry about the dangers of getting emotionally involved. He'd never allow it. Her defences would remain in place. She'd keep herself safe. And it hadn't escaped her that she still hadn't managed to convince him to meet Finn.

Here was a chance to kill several birds with one stone, she thought, a faint stab of guilt piercing the fiery desire that was unfurling in the pit of her stomach and stealing into every part of her. She might never have the opportunity again. 'All right.'

Twenty-four hours later, with the thundering of his heart receding and his breath evening out, Rico stared up at the ceiling of his bedroom, which was still spinning, and congratulated himself once again on the brilliance of his decision to ask Carla to stay. The moment she'd agreed—which had filled him with greater relief than he could ever have imagined the suggestion warranted—he'd rolled her beneath him, and, with the exception of the phone call he'd made half an hour later, they'd barely made it out of his bed since. He was feeling fitter and more energised than he had in ages and he couldn't think of anyone with whom he'd rather make up for the abstinence of the last three months.

'So what are we going to do today?' she murmured huskily, stretching languidly beside him.

'I have an idea,' he said as unbelievably his body began to stir yet again.

She batted him with a pillow. 'I know *I'm* on leave,' she said with a quick grin that for some reason struck him square in the chest like a dart, 'but don't you have to work? What will happen to your billions under management if they're not being managed?'

'But they are.'

'Who by?'

'I hired someone.'

She sat up, to his immense disappointment clutching the sheet to her chest. 'Wow,' she said, staring at him, all tousled and rosy cheeked, which was a very good look on her, and, even better, a look put there by him.

'It makes sense,' he said, not quite sure why the news should provoke quite such surprise.

'I know. But…well…wow. When?'

'Yesterday morning.'

'The phone call?'

'That's right.'

'Who?'

'My nearest competitor. He jumped at the chance to come and work for me and he's extremely keen and exceptionally able. So I'm utterly at your disposal for as long as you want me.'

'Don't worry,' she said lightly. 'I still only want you until Saturday.'

'Of course,' he said smoothly, ignoring the

strangely bitter taste the thought of her departure left in his mouth.

She stared at him for a moment longer, the expression in her eyes unreadable, and then gave her beautiful shoulders a quick shrug. 'Well, we can't keep on doing nothing but having sex.'

'Can't we?'

'I've never been to Venice before. I'd like to see some sights.'

'Plenty to look at here,' he drawled, pulling down the sheet that was draped across him.

'Stop it,' she said with a smile. 'I'm serious. I vaguely recall a plan to learn Italian. I have a hankering to try some proper tiramisu. And even though I haven't had much use for them lately I'm also going to need to buy some new clothes.'

'Va bene,' he said, reflecting that, since he'd given his housekeeper the week off, they probably did need to pick up some supplies. 'If I really can't tempt you back into bed, we will visit the city. Give me an hour to make some arrangements.'

By the time they sat down to lunch in a divine cafe that appeared in no guidebook but apparently served the best tiramisu in the city, Rico had taken Carla on a private tour of the Doge's Palace and had St Mark's Basilica and the Bell Tower closed to the public so that they might ex-plore them in peace and solitude. They'd had an argument about whether biscotti were better on their own or dipped in *vin santo* and a discussion about up to exactly what time it was acceptable to order a cappuccino. The entire morning had been an incredible experience and, for Carla at least, very much needed.

Not for a second had she regretted agreeing to stay with him for a few more days. She'd had no doubts about changing her flight to Saturday morning, which would give her the rest of the weekend back home to prepare for the week ahead and proved that she was still using her head, not her heart, to make decisions. She wouldn't have thought it possible, but instead of lessening in passion and heat, the sex had been only getting better.

But she'd woken up this morning needing a change of scenery. The hours since the moment he'd caved in to the desire he had for her had been incredibly intense, increasingly light on chat and heavy on action. And while she hadn't exactly felt trapped, she'd definitely felt a need for space and a break.

'So you're an exceptionally good tour guide,' she said, taking a sip of her chianti and thinking of the deluge of information he'd presented her with, dates and facts that indicated an encyclopaedic knowledge of the city.

'I've had plenty of practice,' he answered, his eyes shielded by his mirrored shades. 'I know these streets and canals and everything within them like the back of my hand.'

Her head immediately swam with everything he'd told her about his youth, but she pushed it aside because it was far too beautiful a day for an analysis of his distressing past.

'Well, if this person you've hired proves too good and you become surplus to requirements,' she said, thinking instead about how taken aback she'd been by the news that he, who'd always operated totally alone, had taken on the responsibility of an employee, 'at least you know you have an alternative employment option.'

'I won't. I'm excellent at what I do and I need to do it.'

'You're very driven.'

'As are you.'

'Why do you think that is?'

'Probably because if you keep moving forwards at great pace, it's harder for the past to catch up with you.'

'This is true,' she said, tilting her head while she gave it some consideration and came to the conclusion that he could be right. 'Although I'm totally over mine, of course,' she added, thinking of the return of her confidence and self-esteem and the way she'd eventually had sex again, even though it had taken another four years before she'd been brave enough to take the plunge.

'Are you?'

She nodded. 'Endless conversations with Georgie and the therapy my parents arranged worked wonders. You ought to try it.'

His dark eyebrows lifted. 'You had therapy?'

'A lot of it. And counselling. For at least a year. They felt terribly guilty. '

'And so they should.'

'Well, yes,' she admitted, remembering being in plays at school that no one came to and coming top in tests that no one praised her for. 'But they weren't to blame any more than I was. Shortly after I was rescued, they started talking about moving off the commune and adopting a more conventional lifestyle, but I persuaded them out of it. They'd got a bit smothering by that point and I just wanted it behind me.'

'Is that why you don't see much of them?'

'That and distance,' she said with a nod. 'They're now halfway up a hill in Wales.'

'I can see why Georgie means so much to you, even if I don't get it.'

'What don't you get?'

'The depth of your relationship.' He took a sip of his beer and she really wished he'd take off his sunglasses.

'How deep do your relationships go?'

'I don't have any.'

Just as she suspected, she thought, and her heart squeezed at the realisation of how lonely he must be. 'That's a shame.'

'It's never bothered me,' he said with a casual shrug that made her suddenly wonder if she was wrong. Maybe he wasn't lonely at all. Maybe he was perfectly content with his life the way it was. Maybe that was why he had no interest in meeting Finn.

'Well, Georgie and I are closer than sisters,' she said, not entirely sure what to make of that, 'and I owe her a debt I'll never be able to repay.'

'Is that why you accepted my invitation to dinner?'

'Partly,' she said. 'I also needed to assuage my guilt.'

'Your guilt?'

'I allowed you to leave that day. That shouldn't have happened. I should never have left you alone. I made a mistake I'd never normally have made.'

'Then why did you?'

'You threw me off balance.'

'Did I?'

'You must have known you did.'

'You are a master of concealment.'

'Takes one to know one. And, talking of relationships and that afternoon,' she said with a deep breath, not willing to consider the idea that he might genuinely be fine on his own and that her mission might fail, 'have you had any thoughts about meeting Finn?'

'No.'

'Because I really think you should, Rico, and not just because he wants it but because it would be so good for you too.'

'It's none of your business.'

'Well, no, but—'

'Are you trying to ruin the day?'

The smile he gave her was faint, but she could hear a chilly bite to his words. Her throat went dry and her stomach clenched. 'Of course not,' she said, the wine in her system turning to acid.

'Then stop.'

Having got through the rest of lunch with mercifully little conversation, Rico left Carla in the hands of the top personal shopper at the top department store he'd rung earlier, and took himself off to the Capella di Santa Maria, not because he was remotely religious but because he'd always found comfort in the shady coolness of the small but perfectly formed building, and since it wasn't on the tourist trail, which meant it had never been a location for any of his adolescent scams or thievery, it dredged up no memories.

Was there *any* hope of finding comfort now?

With everything crashing around inside him,

it didn't seem likely. He couldn't seem to stop thinking about the support Carla had had in the aftermath of her experience. That kind of help hadn't been made available to him at any point between his parents' death and the moment he'd torn free from gang life. And when he'd been older and it could have become an option, he'd had that part of his life locked away so long he hadn't known where the key even was.

But what if he *had* had access to help? was the thought now ricocheting around his head as he shoved open the heavy oak door and went in. What if he had been able to talk it through with someone who wouldn't have judged but could have helped him make sense of it all? How differently might his life have turned out? Could he have had friends? Could he have had what Finn had? A wife, a child, a family?

And why the hell was he even thinking about it? His instruction to Carla to quit pushing Finn on him could just as easily have been directed at himself, because for some infuriating reason it was becoming harder to put him from his mind too. He didn't *want* what Finn had. Regrets were pointless. Hindsight was something only fools indulged in. Envy, the kind that had sliced through him when Carla had been talking about how fortunate she'd been to have a friend like Georgie, served no purpose whatsoever.

And yet, it struck him suddenly, perhaps he *did* have the chance to talk about it now. With Carla. She was always encouraging him to reveal his secrets and pushing him for answers. What if he trusted her with his past and gave them to her?

No.

That was one reckless move even he couldn't make. He couldn't afford to make connections and allow emotions to invade his life. He didn't want to ever suffer the pain of rejection and abandonment again, or experience the devastation when everything went wrong. The way he'd chosen to live his life, free from exploitation, free from fear, *alone*, was fine.

But what if it wasn't? What if it could be better?

The insidious thoughts slunk into his head and dug in their claws, and his heart began to thump. What if Carla had had a point about no man being an island, even him? He was finding it impossibly difficult to maintain his facade with her, but maybe he ought to simply stop trying. Maybe he ought to let her see the dark, empty man beneath the easy-going surface. She'd been through it. She'd understand. She'd be the last person to judge. And then perhaps he'd be able to ease up on the constant drive for more and find some kind of peace.

All he had to do, he thought, nevertheless sweating at the mere concept of it, was take that risk.

* * *

By the time they'd finished dinner and everything had been cleared away Carla, staring out over the lagoon from the terrace upon which they'd eaten, was unable to stand the tension radiating off Rico any longer.

From the moment they'd left the city, she laden with bags, he carrying a ten-kilo box of groceries as if it weighed nothing, he'd been on edge and distant, as if somewhere else entirely, and it had twisted her stomach into knots.

What was behind it? she'd asked herself all evening, the knots tightening. It couldn't be the amount she'd spent on clothes because she was paying him back, for everything. So was he concerned she was going to continue to try and persuade him to meet his brother again?

Well, he had nothing to fear on that front. She'd gone over it endlessly while trying on outfits, and it had struck her suddenly that she could be flogging a dead horse here, that he might never feel about Finn the way she wanted him to, and perhaps she ought to stop.

And while her heart broke for him, and for Georgie and Finn, if she was being brutally honest, it *was* none of her business. It was between Rico and Finn. Or not. But either way, however great the debt she owed Georgie, she had to let it go, because who was she to tell Rico what to think or what to do? Her family wasn't exactly functional, and what made her an expert on relationships anyway?

She'd blithely told him that she was over what had happened to her, but she'd realised that was a lie. If she was truly over it she wouldn't fear commitment. She wouldn't fear getting swallowed up and losing her identity and her independence. By now she'd have had at least one proper relationship. She might even be married. So she was a big fat fraud and it was time to stop.

Taking a deep breath, Carla slid her gaze from the dark waters of the lagoon and turned to him.

'I'm sorry,' she said quietly, her heart pounding when he met her gaze, his eyes and expression unfathomable.

'What for?'

'Well, firstly for getting my bag stolen and upturning your life this last week. I can tell how hard it's been for you. And secondly, for trying to get you to see the whole Finn thing differently. You've made it very clear that you don't want to discuss it and I haven't respected that. I've been overstepping. Hugely. With the best of intentions, but still. So I apologise.'

For a moment there was silence and then he gave her the faintest of smiles. 'Don't go giving up on me now, Carla.'

Something in his voice lifted the tiny hairs

at the back of her neck and she went very still.
'What do you mean?'

'I was hoping to talk to you.'

'What about?'

'My youth.'

Her heart thudded against her ribs. 'Why?'

'You suggested therapy.'

'I'm no psychologist.'

'But you understand and I trust you and I'd like
your insight. Please.'

The thumping of her pulse intensified and she
went hot with apprehension. He was shedding his
detachment. He'd decided to put his trust in her.
This was the kind of emotional intimacy she'd always striven to avoid. She couldn't get involved.
Yet she already was, she had to acknowledge. She
had been from the moment she'd started pushing
him to open up and answer her questions. And for
him to even think about asking for her insight—
although what made him think she'd have any she
had no idea—must have cost him greatly.

How could she possibly refuse him? Maybe
she *could* help him. Maybe, however unwise it
might turn out to be, she even wanted to. 'I'll
fetch more wine.'

CHAPTER ELEVEN

No AMOUNT OF alcohol was going to make this easier, thought Rico, his heart beating a thunderous tattoo at the realisation that there was no going back from this. But at least it was dark.

'I'm not entirely sure where to start,' he said thickly, once Carla had filled their glasses and set the bottle down on the table.

'Why don't you tell me about your parents?'

Shifting on his seat to ease the discomfort, he forced his mind back to the people he barely remembered. 'My mother was a dentist, my father was an estate agent. From what I can recall, which isn't a lot, we were a small, normal, middle class family.'

'Were you loved?'

He allowed a tiny seam of memory to open up, a hazy blur of hugs and kisses, and felt a ribbon of warmth wind through him. 'Yes.'

'You said they died in a car crash. What happened?'

'I was at school,' he muttered, rubbing his chest as if that might erase the sharp stab of pain. 'A car overtaking on a bend went straight into them. They were killed instantly.'

'And the driver?'

'Him too.'

'So you didn't even get justice.'

Her statement lodged deep and then detonated. 'No,' he said, realising with a start that he'd never thought about in that way even though it was an obvious explanation for the intense anger he'd felt at the time. 'I got no closure at all. I had no time to process the shock or the grief before I was taken into care. It was like I'd been hurled off a moving ship and into a heaving, churning sea.'

'I can't begin to imagine,' she said softly, her voice catching.

'I was so lost and so alone. I'd been ripped apart from everything I'd ever known and tossed into a whole new world. A new school, new faces, a new home. Except none of the places I lived in were home. There was nothing wrong with them, it was just that I quickly learned that wherever I was sent was only ever going to be temporary and so to make attachments would be pointless. I realised I belonged nowhere and I ran away to find something better.' He gave a bitter laugh and shook his head. 'If only I'd known... *Dio*, the fear...the hunger...'

'So the gang became your family.'

'That was what I'd hoped,' he said, for a moment losing himself in the sympathy he could see in her gaze and feeling the ribbon of warmth begin to unfurl and spread. 'I was so excited about it. I genuinely thought I'd found a place to belong, but I was swiftly disabused of that too.'

'In what way?'

'There was no loyalty,' he said, his chest tightening as the memory of the shock, bewilderment and finally devastation flashed into his head. 'No code of honour. I was just useful and light-fingered and suited their purposes. And then when I was arrested and therefore no longer of any use they were nowhere to be seen, which is why I took the job.'

'That must have been devastating to discover,' she said softly, her eyes clouding in the candle-light.

'It was. I put my trust in the wrong people and I allowed myself to be exploited. But by the time I realised what was going on I was in too deep to get out.'

'You said you were responsible for the accounting,' she said, her eyes fixed to his.

'I was good with figures. They didn't care that I was only fifteen. They put me in charge of cleaning the money and collecting the debts. I was handy with my fists and big for my age.

One time I nearly put a man in hospital. I carry the shame and guilt of every dirty, terrible thing I did to this day.'

'You were so young.'

'But old enough to know right from wrong.'

'None of it was your fault.'

'Wasn't it?'

'No,' she said vehemently, sitting up and leaning forwards, the sudden burn in her eyes scything through the numb chill he'd lived with for so long. 'Your parents' death was a tragedy, and there was nothing anyone could have done about that, but you were let down by a whole host of people who should have done more. You were what, eleven, twelve, when you started running away?'

'About that.'

'They should have tried harder. Someone should have fought for you. You should not have been allowed to slip through the net.'

Maybe she was right, he thought, the tension gripping his body easing a fraction. He'd been little more than a child. He'd been dealt an impossibly tough hand and he'd had no idea how to play it.

'And as for your later actions,' she continued in the same fierce tone, 'I suspect you've been trying to atone for them ever since.'

'What makes you say that?'

'The donation to the consul's wife's charity for homeless children. What other charities do you support, Rico?'

Plenty. Anonymously where possible and always at a distance. 'A few.'

'I thought so. I bet you've done an immense amount of good over the years.'

'It will never be enough.'

'You have to forgive yourself.'

'That's easier said than done.'

'But not impossible. If I can, you can.'

He frowned. 'I thought you said you knew you weren't to blame.'

'That was after the therapy,' she said. 'Initially, I blamed everyone for what happened to me but the person responsible. I was livid at having been discovered. I'd considered myself so sophisticated, so much more interesting and mature than everyone else. I accused Georgie of being jealous and my parents of not wanting me to be happy. When the scales finally fell from my eyes, thanks to the therapy, I felt like the biggest fool in the world. I hated that he'd had the power to do that to me and that I'd been so easy to manipulate. I swore that I would never allow it to happen again, and it hasn't. So I know all about shame and guilt and grubbiness.'

'You're beautiful.'

'In this old thing?'

'You are the most beautiful woman I've ever met.' And the strongest. Whereas he felt utterly weak and drained. The ground beneath his feet was unstable and he suddenly felt strangely adrift, which was why he turned his attention to something he could hold on to, something he did understand. 'Let's go to bed.'

Rico did an excellent job of attempting to wear Carla out, but while he slumbered away on the bed, of which he now seemed to hog less and upon which he now barely twitched, sleep eluded her.

While she sat on the balcony watching the sparkle of moonlight on the water, their conversation ran through her head as if on a never-ending loop, the details of which she didn't think she'd ever forget.

Her throat closed and her eyes prickled just to think about it. Her heart was in tatters for the boy he'd been, for all the children all over the world who one way or another slipped through the net. She couldn't imagine the loneliness he must have felt. The terror and the confusion and the hunger, the fear of which he still clearly carried with him. And all the while struggling to come to terms with the death of his parents.

His detachment and desire to move through life on his own made so much sense now. No wonder he kept himself apart and relied on no one but himself. No wonder he didn't form attachments when he'd experienced the destruction they could bring. She could totally understand why he didn't want to look back and why he had no mementos of the past he'd spent a long time trying to forget. He'd been exploited and abused, manipulated and badly let down. Who'd want to remember that?

How on earth had he had the strength to survive? she wondered, her chest tightening as she tried and failed to imagine the horror and brutality he'd been a part of. She'd always thought that she'd had a rough time of growing up, but compared to his experiences, hers had been a walk in the park. She'd had people looking out for her, even if she hadn't appreciated it at the time. Rico had undergone hell and, with the exception of the judge who'd given him a way out, had had no one on his side, no one fighting his corner.

He'd learned how to hide it, and hide it well, but once upon a time he'd been as vulnerable as her and just as easy to prey upon. He knew as well as she did what it was like to be manipulated and exploited. Was that why she had the feeling that he instinctively got her? Was that why when he called her beautiful she didn't inwardly cringe as usual but deep down purred instead? Compliments, which could be flimsy, easily given and weren't to be trusted, had always made her uncomfortable, but when they came from Rico—was she really the most beautiful woman he'd ever met?—they made her melt.

In fact, she thought, something in her chest shifting and settling, everything about him made her melt. His strength. His resilience. His innate if reluctant chivalry and the way he'd taken care of her after her bag had been stolen, even though she'd resisted with every bone in her body.

Even if he couldn't figure out what the judge had seen in him, she could. She saw a frightened, grieving child who'd found himself in a situation of indescribable torment. She saw an indomitable will to survive by any means necessary, and the inherent good that had made him the incredible man he was today.

'What are you doing out here?'

His deep, rumbling voice broke into her swirling thoughts and she turned to see him standing in the doorway wearing nothing but a white towel wrapped around his waist.

Feeling strangely giddy, her heart thumping unusually fast, Carla got to her feet and undid the belt of her robe. She didn't want to talk. She didn't want to dwell on the way the foundations of her existence seemed to be shifting. She just wanted to feel. So she put a hand on his chest and gave him a little push and they tangoed back until he was lying on the bed and she was straddling him, his towel having been discarded en route.

Without a word she leaned down, put her hands on his head and sealed her mouth to his. She kissed him hard and long, her pulse pounding and desire throbbing deep inside her. He clamped one big, strong hand on her hip and the other at the back of her neck, his palms like a brand on her heated skin.

Tearing her mouth from his, her chest heaving and her breath coming in pants, she dotted a trail of tiny kisses down the column of his throat, the hard-muscled expanse of his chest, her heart thumping as she took extra care with his scars, and then lower, over the ridges of his abdomen, shimmying down his body until she reached his long, hard erection, steel encased in velvet.

She could feel the tremors gripping his large frame and when she wrapped her fingers round the base of him and her lips around the tip the groan that tore from his mouth sent reciprocal shivers shooting up and down her spine. She took him deeper into her mouth and his hands moved to her head, threading through her hair, holding her when he needed her, guiding her yet giving her the freedom to use her hands, her mouth and her tongue to drive him to the point where his hips were jerking and his breathing was harsh, his control clearly unravelling.

And then he was lifting her off him and rolling her over, applying a condom and sliding into her with one long, hard, smooth thrust, lodging deep inside her, and staring into her eyes as if trying to see into her soul.

She clung on to him, her gaze locked with his as he began to move, slowly, steadily, driving into her, pushing her higher and higher each time, making her shatter once, white lights flashing in her head, and then again, and again, before with a great groan he buried himself hard and deep and poured into her.

She was wrung out physically and emotionally and her last drowsy thought before she finally fell asleep was, *I could stay here with him for ever.*

At the helm of his boat, with Carla sitting in the stern, Rico was feeling lighter than he had in years yet at the same time oddly uneasy, as if the world had been broken up and put back together with the pieces in the wrong place.

Something had shifted inside him last night, he thought, the frown that he felt he'd been wearing all morning deepening as he increased the throttle and they sped off in the direction of the island of Murano. With her insight and understanding Carla had sliced through his long-held doubts and shone a light on his darkest fears. She'd somehow given him permission to let go of the shame and the guilt he'd carried around for so long—even if he didn't think he could let it go just yet—and he had the strange sensation that tiny droplets of light might slowly be beginning to drip into the great well of nothingness inside him.

But he'd sensed something change in her too and that was the source of his discomfort. The shimmering emotion he'd seen in her gaze when he'd found her on the balcony, before she'd subsequently blown his mind, wasn't something he'd needed to witness. He didn't want her pity or her sympathy. He didn't want anything more with her than what he already had.

But it was what *she* might want that was his concern. He'd assumed she was on board with the temporary nature of their arrangement, but what if for some reason what they had now became not enough for her? What if she wound up wanting more? Under no circumstances could he allow that to happen. He'd never be able to give her more, no matter how much talking they did. He'd been on his own for so long it simply wasn't in him. But he would never want to hurt Carla, so he had to prevent such a situation arising at all costs and nip things in the bud before they got out of control.

And not only for her benefit, he forced himself to acknowledge.

Yesterday while he'd been showing her the

sights he'd started to see his city through her eyes and it had been illuminating. He'd noticed less of the grey and the grime and more of the glitter and shine. Colours had seemed strangely brighter, sounds sharper, smells more intense. Even the heat, which he was well used to and had not changed, felt fiercer.

This shifting of the sands over unstable ground couldn't continue. A stronger-willed man would send Carla home now, and retreat to rebuild his walls, but he wasn't a stronger-willed man. He was a man who wanted her in his bed for as long as they had left. He just had to keep reminding himself that great sex was all it was.

The island of Murano, famed for its glass and a stone's throw from Venice, was amazing. Far less busy than its much bigger neighbour, it had colourful low-rise houses, wide, tranquil canals and a laid-back vibe that made Carla want to stop and linger along the walkways so she might have time to take it all in.

Vibrant glass sculptures stood in piazzas, glinting and sparkling in the midday sun. Rico had taken her to a workshop off the beaten track where she'd spent a good half an hour watching a glassblower creating a vase. She'd even picked up a bauble of her own.

The only minor awkward moment came when,

while strolling down a walkway beside him, she'd suddenly been overwhelmed by the romance of it all, giddy with the effect this man had on her, and had reached for his hand, only to feel him jerk it away when her fingers brushed his.

'After all this,' said Carla, hiding her mortification behind a bright smile and determinedly reminding herself that she didn't, ever, do romance and, more importantly, neither did he. 'London's going to feel very pedestrian.'

'But it's your home.'

'It is and it's great,' she said, thinking that she really *did* love it with all its energy and buzz and variety, and she really *was* looking forward to getting back to it. 'But this is beautiful and Venice is stunning. Everywhere you turn there's another incredible piece of architecture and it's such... I don't know...an *effervescent* city.'

'And unfortunately,' he said drily, 'sinking.'

'So I've read. Why's that happening?'

'Early settlers drained the lagoon, dug canals and shored up banks by piling tree trunks into the silt. They laid great wooden platforms on top of the piles and stone on top of that and started building from there. But increased traffic in the canals—not to mention the cruise ships—has started churning up the water and the silt and the trunks are being exposed to oxygen that's making them rot. There's a campaign to ban everything but gondolas and small boats and it has my full backing.'

She knew how Venice felt, she thought dreamily, wondering for a moment what it would be like to be fought for like that. She too had been fine for years and then stirred up and exposed. She too had the sensation she was slowly sinking into deeper waters than felt safe, only in her case there was no one there to save her.

'You care,' she said, focusing on the topic of conversation and not the sliver of worry that slid through her at the thought that even though she'd done her best to prevent it she might be getting involved.

'It's complicated.'

'It's your home.'

'It was also my prison.'

'It's shaped the man you are and it's in your blood. I can't imagine you living anywhere else.'

'Neither can I. Can you imagine living anywhere other than London?'

Yes. She could imagine living here. With him. All too easily. But, despite what she'd thought last night, addled with emotions, this wasn't for forever. 'No,' she said, because it was the only answer she could give and anything else was simply not possible. 'As you pointed out, it's my home. I can't wait to get back.'

'Tomorrow's your last day,' he said, his eyes

fixed on hers but curiously devoid of anything. 'What would you like to do?'

'I think I'd like to learn to pilot a gondola,' she said, struggling to ignore the tightening of her chest at the thought of leaving, determined instead to make the most of what little time she had left.

'Your wish is my command.'

But if only her wish *was* his command, thought Carla wistfully the next day, perching on the padded bench seat as Rico steered the *batela* through the busy and choppy canals and out into the relative calm of a more placid section of the lagoon. Because she was beginning to wish she hadn't been quite so sensible in booking a flight for tomorrow morning. She didn't need a whole day and a half to prepare to go back to work. She'd only been on leave for a week. What *had* she been thinking?

'I thought I was going to be learning to pilot a gondola,' she said, looking up at him, so breathtakingly gorgeous her heart turned over.

'Patience,' he said with the arch of one dark eyebrow. 'A gondola is a very technical boat. Tourists start on these.'

'And is that what I am? A tourist?'

'What else would you be?'

It was a question to which she didn't have an

answer, even after an hour's tuition that took two, since shortly after it had begun there'd been a rocky moment during which she'd needed close contact support and her concentration had fled.

She was none the wiser when he handed her the oar and murmured, 'Your turn now,' or when she arched an eyebrow, gave him a wide grin from her position at the front of the boat and asked, 'Do you trust me?'

It was only when he replied, 'You already know I do,' with a smile so blinding, so real, that it lit up his face and stole her breath, which weakened her knees, robbed her of her balance and promptly toppled her headlong into the lagoon, that she realised she was head over heels in love with him.

Rico had dived straight in after her. By the time he'd hauled himself back onto the boat and then pulled her up too, the coastguard had arrived. An hour later, with the paperwork completed and tetanus shots administered, they'd been delivered back to his island, where they'd got out of their wet things and taken a scalding shower.

Carla had been unusually quiet for the rest of the evening. No doubt, she was still in shock. He knew he was. He didn't think he'd ever forget the moment she'd fallen into the water. Time had slowed right down, but the sheer terror that had ripped through him, wilder than any tide, had been swift and immense. She'd gone under for the briefest of seconds, but to him it had felt like a lifetime. He hadn't thought twice about diving in to rescue her. The only thought screaming through his head was that he couldn't lose her.

And that was equally terrifying.

She wasn't his to lose. Or keep. She never would be. She was leaving in the morning and going home. He was going to wave her off with no regrets, and reclaim the life he'd led before the accident had blown it apart. That was the plan and it was a good one, a necessary one.

Nevertheless, when he held her in his arms in bed that night he did so a little more tightly. He found himself noting every sound she uttered, every move she made, and storing them somewhere safe. And when he moved inside her, he realised he was trembling.

'Are you all right?' she asked softly, once the sweat had cooled on their skin and their harsh, heavy breathing had faded.

'I'm fine,' he said, but he wasn't. He didn't know what was wrong with him. All he knew was that he wasn't fine at all.

CHAPTER TWELVE

ON THE MORNING of her departure, while Rico was in the shower Carla was methodically folding and putting clothes into the suitcase she'd had to buy to accommodate her recent purchases. But if anyone had asked her to itemise those clothes, she'd have merely blinked in bewilderment.

The drenching she'd had yesterday afternoon had been an almighty shock but not nearly as great as the one that had led to it. Ever since, she'd been able to think of nothing but the stunning realisation she was in love with Rico.

Which couldn't possibly be.

She'd known him for less than a week. She didn't know what love was. Not this kind of love. She loved Georgie, of course, and even her parents, despite all their flaws, but this was entirely different. This was…well, she didn't know what this was.

And yet all these feelings, which had been rushing around inside her for a while but now flooded her like a tsunami, had to mean something. Why else would her heart tighten every time she thought of what he'd been through? Why else would she overflow with admiration and respect at what he'd achieved? He was the only person she wanted to talk to. The only person alive she wanted to tell everything to and find out everything about. He'd become her world. He'd even saved her from sinking.

So much for steering clear of emotional intimacy, she thought, her pulse pounding and her head spinning as she distractedly packed. She'd been creating it and encouraging it since the moment she'd met him.

And had that been such a bad thing?

No.

Quite the opposite in fact.

He'd shown her that ceding emotional ground didn't have to lead to vulnerability and weakness. It could actually lead to empowerment and healing instead. He'd shown her what a proper relationship could look like, free from manipulation and fear. How it could be a give and take of ideas and opinions, an exchange of thoughts and experiences, hopes and dreams, and not a loss of identity. He'd given her space. He'd given her choice. If this was love, then she adored him, and when she focused on the happiness beginning to spread through her like sunshine, it was glorious.

When she thought of what Georgie had it didn't fill her with horror, it filled her with envy. When she thought of combining a family with a career she realised it was a challenge she'd be thrilled to embrace.

Could she dare to hope that Rico had reached a similar conclusion and now felt the same way? she wondered, her throat dry and heart thudding wildly as he took her cases downstairs and loaded up the boat.

Like her he'd said little since her dip in the lagoon, but somehow she sensed that, like her, he'd changed. He'd dropped his facade and shown her the whole of the man beneath. He'd opened up to her. He'd told her things she didn't think he'd told anyone ever before. He'd trusted her with his past and his soul. Despite his reluctance, he'd let her into his sanctuary, into his life. That had to have meant something.

And then, the tenderness with which he'd made love to her last night… That had definitely been new, as was the glittering warmth with which she'd caught him looking at her on several occasions over the last couple of days.

There was so much to this amazing, complex, beautiful man, she thought dizzily as they sped across the lagoon towards the airport, the exhilarating rush of wind blowing through her body and whipping up a storm inside her. So much more that she longed to know. She wanted to talk with him, make love with him and fight his corner, today, tomorrow, for ever.

So what happened now? Time was running out. All too soon the airport hove into view and then he was slowing the engine of the boat and tossing a loop of rope over a mooring post.

Did she dare hope he might, like her, want more? Might he ask her to stay the rest of the weekend? What would she do if he did? What would she do if he didn't? Was she brave enough to take the initiative herself? Was she ready to take the greatest risk of her life?

Oh, this was *awful*.

Having deposited her bags on the jetty, Rico helped her off the boat and pushed his sunglasses up onto his head. 'Well, here we are,' he said, his voice giving away absolutely nothing.

'Do you mind if I send your phone back in a day or two?' she said, her stomach churning with nerves while her heart hammered frantically. 'It has my boarding pass on it.'

'Keep it as long as you need.'

'I'll put it in the post as soon as I get home and I'll transfer the money I owe you.'

'Fine.'

He looked as if he was going to take a step back and her throat went tight.

'I bought you something,' she said in a rush,

swallowing hard as she dug around in her new handbag for the gift she'd seen and impulsively bought for him the day before yesterday. 'A gift. A kitsch gift, admittedly, and one that was technically bought with your money, but still, here.'

She handed it to him, her fingers brushing against his, which made her heart leap for a moment and then plunge when he frowned.

'What is it?'

'A fridge magnet. I picked it up in Murano.' She'd seen it and been amused by it and had a vivid vision of it actually on the door of his fridge, the only personal possession on show in his house.

He stared at the scene of his city, complete with canal, bridge and gondola, depicted in appallingly rendered relief above a bright red 'Venezia', as if he'd never seen such a horrendous thing in his life and had no idea what to do with it, which instantly made her regret her decision to give it to him.

'*Grazie,*' he muttered, eventually slipping it into his pocket, since clearly there was nowhere else for it to go.

'It's I who should be thanking you,' she said, wishing fervently she'd never bought it in the first place and covering her embarrassment with a shaky smile. 'It's been quite a week.'

'It has indeed.'

For a moment he just looked at her while she willed him to ask her to stay, but he remained resolutely silent, so she took a deep breath and before her courage could desert her said, 'I wondered if maybe you'd like to meet for dinner in London, next time you're there.'

He froze. For the briefest of seconds she thought she caught a glimpse of pleasure light the depths of his eyes, but it was gone in a flash and there instead was the cool indifference she'd thought long gone. 'I'm not planning on a trip any time soon,' he said, with a return to the drawl she hated.

'Maybe I'll find myself back in Venice some time,' she said doggedly. 'Maybe I'll look you up instead.'

'You'd be wasting your time. There'd be nothing waiting for you here.'

The flatness of his tone struck her square in the chest, knocking the breath from her lungs, and she reeled. Where had the man she'd fallen in love with gone? Where was the smile and the warmth?

'Are you sure?' she said, her voice cracking a little in response to the ice she could feel forming inside him.

'Quite sure.'

His expression was unreadable and his eyes were devoid of every emotion in existence, but his meaning couldn't be any clearer. For whatever reason, he didn't want her the way she wanted him and it was agony.

'Right. No. Of course not. Sorry,' she said, a thousand tiny darts stabbing at her chest.

'We agreed a week.'

'I know.'

'I'm sorry I can't give you what you want, Carla.'

Couldn't? Or wouldn't? She wasn't going to ask. There was only so much humiliation she could bear. 'It's fine,' she said, dredging up a smile from who knew where because she was not going to fall apart in front of him, however much it cost her. 'It's not your fault I fell in love with you.' The almost imperceptible widening of his eyes was the only indication he'd heard what she'd said. Other than that he remained silent, his face expressionless. 'None of this is your fault,' she continued. It was hers. All hers. She was the one who'd read too much into everything and come to conclusions that didn't exist. However much it broke her heart, he might never be ready to embrace everything she and life had to offer and there was nothing she could do about it. 'I just have one last request,' she said shakily, determined that *some* good should come of this.

'Name it.'

'I know I can't force you to see things my way

about getting to know Finn, but you've been looking for a family, Rico, and you have one. A great one. Please say you'll at least think about meeting him. At least give me that.'

For the longest of moments he didn't say anything—was he really going to make her beg, after everything?—but then he gave a short nod. '*Va bene,*' he said. 'I can give you that. I'll think about it.'

'Thank you.'

And with her heart in bits, her body aching with sadness and disappointment, the warmth of the day and the sunshine beating down on her a bitter contrast to the chill seeping into her bones and the darkness now enveloping her like a heavy black cloud, Carla turned on her heel and walked away.

With every step she took the strength leached from her limbs, but despite the stinging of her eyes and the sobs building in her chest she held it together through Check-in. She made her way through Security and Passport Control without giving in to the pain clawing at her stomach and shredding her heart.

It was only once she was on the plane and in the air and Rico hadn't made a dramatic appearance to declare his love for her and beg her to stay—as she'd secretly, *stupidly*, been hoping—that her defences exploded and she crumbled.

How could she have got it so wrong? she thought desperately, tears leaking out of her eyes and rolling down her cheeks as she stared out of the window, her heart breaking at the realisation that with every second she was leaving him behind. She'd been so sure. He'd taken on an employee in order to spend more time with her. He'd sought her counsel and shared intimate details of his past. He—a man who had spent so long on his own—had let her into his world.

But she *hadn't* got it wrong, she told herself, nudging her sunglasses out of the way so she could wipe her eyes with a tissue as she went over the conversation for the hundredth time. He'd been tempted to say yes to dinner. He'd wanted to embrace everything she'd offered. She'd felt it. So why the resistance? Why didn't he want to fight for her the way she wanted to fight for him? Why was his attachment to the past more important than a future with her? Why wasn't she enough? Why wouldn't he allow himself to love her?

She'd taken the biggest gamble of her life, she realised, the pain slicing through her and splitting her wide open unlike any she'd felt before, and she'd lost. What was she going to do?

* * *

Rico spent the first day following Carla's departure once again thanking God at having had such a lucky escape. He'd been right to recognise the danger of her wanting more. He'd been right to reject her offer of dinner in London.

But as the relief faded the guilt set in. That she'd fallen in love with him was his fault. He should have put a stop to it sooner. He should have resisted her allure. He should never have opened up to her. He should never have let her into his life in the first place.

The rampant remorse sent him to his gym, where he tried to sweat out the image of how devastated she'd looked when he'd said there was nothing left for her here, which seemed to be permanently etched into his memory. He'd hurt her further when she'd declared she was in love with him and he hadn't said a word, he realised grimly as he rowed a stretch of the Arno on the ergometer, his muscles screaming with every stroke. He'd done more than that. He'd crushed her. But who the hell fell in love in a week?

If only he could remove her from his head as decisively as he'd removed her from his home. He didn't want her hanging around in there with her smiles and her warmth. It shouldn't have even been hard to do. It wasn't as if she'd left anything behind apart from that *maledetto* fridge magnet that was hideous and served no purpose and which he should have tossed in the bin instead of slapping it on the door of his fridge and then doing his best to ignore it. He'd never wanted reminders of the past, he was all about looking forward, and he'd never understood why people grew so attached to things.

Carla definitely fell into the category of 'the past' yet annoyingly, *frustratingly*, his house was full of her. Everywhere he looked he could see her, especially in his bedroom, and the images that bombarded him were as vivid as they were unsettling. The villa felt strangely empty without her and when he wasn't on the treadmill, running up and down virtual hills and pounding along virtual paths through virtual valleys and villages, he prowled around it, oddly restless and unpleasantly on edge. Being alone had never bothered him before. It was irritating and frustrating that it did now. He didn't even have much work to distract him, since the fund manager he'd hired was so keen to impress.

Unable to stand it any longer, Rico went to Milan to visit a client. The fact that the city was also home to the law firm where his parents had lodged their letter to him all those years ago was not a coincidence.

Because when he wasn't remonstrating with himself about how badly he'd handled Carla and regretting the promise guilt had forced him to make, he found he couldn't stop thinking about these brothers of his, the family he might have out there. Long before he'd met her and lost his mind, Finn at least had been lurking in the depths of his conscience, unwelcome and unacknowledged but nevertheless there.

Rico remembered all too clearly how he'd felt when he'd first seen the picture of his brother in the press, the sense of something missing slipping into place. Carla had been right about that, and although it pained him to admit it he was beginning to wonder if she might have been right about other things. Such as the importance and the significance of family. The basic human need for connection. He'd always operated alone and relied solely on himself—he'd even found having to put himself in the hands of medical experts in the aftermath of his accident frustrating and annoying—but perhaps that was what he'd subconsciously been seeking while taking ever-increasing risks and continually pushing himself to do and be more. Maybe that was what he'd always wanted but had been too wary of being exploited and used again to actually reach out and grab. And so perhaps it wasn't the accident on its own that had affected him, but seeing the photo of Finn in conjunction with it.

Rico had never been bothered by the idea of his

own mortality, but it looked as if he was now. He didn't want to die alone in some mountain range. He didn't want to die full stop. His nihilistic approach to life no longer appealed. He didn't want to just fill the days with things that would merely pass the time. Risks now needed to be calculated and recklessness curtailed. He wanted to *live*.

And if everything now running through his head was quite possibly true, then wouldn't it be a good idea to establish contact with Finn? Couldn't he do with allowing someone else into his life and vice versa? How would he know if the gaping void where his soul should be could be filled if he didn't give it a chance?

At least if Finn had been searching for him for months, the likelihood of being rejected by him was low. His brother's email, which had been lurking in his inbox, repeatedly snagging his attention until he'd had no option but to open it and which had contained an invitation to visit at any time, had certainly been encouraging.

Actually meeting his brother needn't open the can of worms he'd feared, he told himself repeatedly. And even if it did, what made him automatically assume he wouldn't be able to handle it? Wasn't it a bit cowardly to keep hiding himself away under the pretext of being better off alone? Was *anyone* better off wholly alone and cut off?

Well, he was about to find out.

Exactly two weeks after he'd first made the trip here, Rico found himself once more at Finn Calvert's door. Not skulking beneath a tree, but actually on the doorstep, on another Saturday afternoon in June.

For a moment he stood there, stock still, his heart thumping so hard and fast it reverberated in his ears, his every muscle tight with tension, anticipation and trepidation. Despite his efforts to downplay the significance of what was about to happen, it was huge. With every passing second his brother and a life irrevocably changed came that bit closer. If he wanted to, this was his last chance to walk away. But he didn't. He was done with the life he used to lead. He and Finn had an appointment and this time he was going to keep it.

And it would be fine, Rico assured himself, taking a deep breath and stiffening his spine as he banged the huge brass knocker twice against the door. This brother of his dominated the hospitality industry and one didn't get to a position like that by being sentimental. There wouldn't be an overload of emotion. No one needed that. And in the unlikely event a heart-to-heart *did* appear to be in the offing, if things moved too fast all he had to do was deflect it and slow them down.

The seconds ticked interminably by, and then came the sound of footsteps, just about audible above the thunder of his pulse. The latch lifted and the door swung open and there, on the other side of the threshold, stood his brother. His *identical* brother, physically at least, bar a few superficial differences. He'd been right about that. Expecting it, even, given how long he'd spent looking at the photo over the last couple of days.

What he hadn't been expecting, however, was the sense of recognition that suddenly slammed into him, smashing through his exterior and striking at his marrow, crushing the air from his lungs and leeching the strength from his knees.

Staring into his brother's eyes was like looking in on himself. The urge to stride over and give him a hug roared up through him, along with the sudden extraordinary concern that Finn might not like him, none of which made any sense, when he hadn't hugged anyone in over twenty years and it didn't matter what Finn thought of him.

'Federico Rossi,' he said, getting a grip of the emotions running riot inside him and holding out a hand to forestall any attempt at something closer from the man who was staring back at him with a gaze containing just as much shock and curiosity that his own had to have. 'Rico.'

'Finn Calvert,' his brother said, taking it. 'Come in.'

'*Grazie,*' he replied, glancing down at the familiar fingers gripping his with similar strength for a moment before forcing himself to let go.

'You have no idea how pleased I am to meet you,' said Finn, breaking into an enviably easy, genuine smile as he stood back to allow Rico to pass. 'I've been looking for you for months. I thought Carla was mad when she told us she was going to Venice to get you to change your mind, but I can't deny I'm glad it worked.'

His heart lurched at the mention of her name, but he swiftly contained it and got a grip. 'How much did she tell you about me?'

'Not a lot. A few basic facts. She said she hadn't got very far.'

She'd got very far indeed. Too far. At which point he'd pushed her away. Which had been absolutely the right thing to do. He had no business wondering how she'd been, he reminded himself, biting back the question on the tip of his tongue. No business knowing he didn't deserve her loyalty but being inexplicably pleased he had it anyway.

'But she did mention that we were identical.'

'Not quite,' Rico replied, snapping himself out of it and forcing himself to focus.

'No. How did you get the scars?'

'A misspent youth.'

'I look forward to hearing all about it,' Finn said, opening the door to the study that only a fortnight ago had put the fear of God into Rico, and heading on in. 'I had one of those briefly. Drink?'

'Sure.'

'Take a seat.'

'Thank you.'

Selecting one of the two wing-backed arm-chairs in front of the fireplace, Rico sat down and glanced around. Strange to think that this room with all its photos had once had him running for the hills, while today he could take it all in with relative equanimity, even if the sight of so much clutter was making him inwardly wince. Even stranger to think that where once he'd had no interest in his brother, now he could barely contain the curiosity ripping through him. The force with which questions were ricocheting around his head, multiplying with every second, was making his pulse race.

'How do you feel about milk?' said Finn, bending down at the sideboard and opening a cupboard.

'It makes me want to throw up,' Rico said, willing everything inside him to calm down so he could process it.

'Me too. We'd better stick to Scotch.'

'Fine with me.'

Finn took a moment to fix the drinks, then handed Rico a generously filled glass and sat in the chair opposite. 'So what made you change your mind about meeting me? You disappeared pretty quickly the last time you were here.'

'I wasn't prepared.'

'But you are now?'

'Not entirely.'

For a moment his brother just looked at him in shrewd understanding. 'I can appreciate that. When I discovered I was adopted—and that I had siblings I knew nothing about—it turned my world upside down.'

'In what way?'

'In pretty much every way. Everything I thought I knew had been a lie. Or that was what I believed, at least.'

'You don't now?'

'Thanks to Georgie, no.'

Another woman with undue influence, although Finn didn't seem particularly bothered by it. Judging by the smile playing at his mouth and the softening of his expression, he didn't mind at all. And perhaps his brother's life had been as gilded as he'd assumed.

'I came because of this.' Reaching into the top pocket on the inside of his jacket, Rico withdrew the letter he'd picked up from the solicitors only yesterday. As if having his thoughts dominated by Carla and Finn wasn't frustrating enough, he hadn't been able to stop thinking about that either, wondering now what it might contain, whether it might somehow be useful. He'd had to find out if it still existed before he drove himself mad. To both his astonishment and that of the archivist, it had been found in a file in a box in the basement.

'What is it?'

'A letter left for me by my adoptive parents to be read at the age of eighteen.'

'And did you read it?'

'Not then. I have now.'

'What does it say?'

Rico didn't have to look at it to remind himself of its contents. He knew every word off by heart. It was a letter penned by his mother and filled with love. She'd written about how much she and his father loved him and always would, but if he ever wanted to look for his birth parents, they'd understand and he should start here. He had broken down when he'd read it. The anger, grief and regret that he'd never had a chance to process had slammed into him and he'd sunk to the floor, racked with so much torment and pain that it had taken hours to blow itself out.

'It gives the name of the agency my parents used to adopt me,' he said gruffly.

'Would you mind if I gave that information to the investigator I have working on the case?'

'Not at all.'

'Thank you.'

'No problem.'

'And how would you feel about doing a joint interview?'

'What kind of an interview?'

'The kind that might go viral and be seen by our elusive third brother.'

It would mean stepping out of the shadows, Rico thought with a faint frown as he rubbed his chest and briefly wondered at the absence of the cold sweat he might have expected at the idea. It would mean a rejection of the past and embracing the future.

But perhaps that was all right.

He'd once thought his life didn't need changing, but he could see now that it most definitely did. His life before Carla had blown into it like a whirlwind had been terrible. A cold, empty desert, devoid of colour and light and warmth. For the week he'd shared it with her, it had been brighter and shinier and better.

She'd shown him what it could be like to let someone in. When he thought about the void he'd lived with for so long, he couldn't find it. She'd filled it with promise and hope. She'd helped put him back together. She'd risen to his defence. She'd never once been anything other than honest and upfront with him. She'd given him her love and her loyalty, even after everything she'd been through, and what had he done?

Still determined to believe that he could only survive if he remained alone, he'd sent her away.

What he'd lost hit him then with the force of a battering ram, slamming into the mile-high walls he'd spent years constructing and reducing them to rubble and dust.

Carla, with her unassailable belief in family and friends, was everything he'd never known he wanted, he realised, his head pounding with the realisations now raining down on him. Everything he'd been subconsciously seeking his entire life while convincing himself that he wasn't lonely and he didn't need anyone. She was strong and brave and tough. And, *Dio*, the loyalty she so fiercely believed in... He'd been on the receiving end of that and it had been stunning.

He'd had the chance to build a future with someone who understood him and who he understood. After years of searching he'd finally found a place to belong and develop new foundations upon which, with her, he could have built a life, something brilliant and strong.

How could he have been such a fool?

Well, he was done with allowing his preoccupation with the past to influence his present. He'd let it dictate his thoughts, his behaviour and his actions for too long. Carla had shown him a glimpse of what his life could be if he took a risk and spent it with her.

And taking the risk was exactly what he was going to do, because as he looked briefly around Finn's study he realised that he wanted the photos. He wanted what Finn had. All of it. And he wanted it with Carla. Seven days ago he'd wondered who the hell fell in love in a week. Well, apparently, he thought, giving free rein to the emotions that had been clamouring for acknowledgement for days and letting them buffet him, that would be him.

'Fix up the interview,' he said, his heart banging so hard against his ribs he feared one might crack. 'It's a good idea.'

'It was Carla's.'

Of course it was. All the good ideas were hers.

'Would you mind if we continued this conversation another time?' he said, leaping to his feet as if the chair were on fire. 'There's somewhere I have to be.'

CHAPTER THIRTEEN

CARLA SAT AT the table on her tiny roof terrace, the glass of rosé before her untouched and the rays of the setting sun doing little to warm the chill she felt deep inside her that just wouldn't shift.

When was it going to stop? she wondered with a sniff. When was the pain going to go away?

She'd done her best to keep herself busy over the last seven days. Unable to face work when she was liable to burst into tears without warning, she'd requested another week's leave. She'd gone to Wales to talk to her parents because in the midst of her agony it had struck her that she'd never told them she didn't hold them responsible for what had happened to her and she'd needed to rectify that. There'd been conversation and hugs and even more tears and she'd invited them to come and stay any time before leaving, feeling as if a great weight had lifted from her shoulders.

If only the same could be said for the weight in her heart.

She'd tried so hard to talk herself out of her feelings for Rico. She'd been one hundred per cent mistaken in her conviction he did feel something for her, she'd told herself resolutely. She'd had no indication that what they'd shared had been anything other than casual. He'd considered her a tourist, someone who by definition was transient. For all she knew, he shared his past with all his lovers. She might be the only one he'd ever invited to stay on his island but that had just been circumstance. She hadn't been special and she'd been a fool to think otherwise.

But even if she had been special, none of it had been real. For the brief period they'd been together, they'd existed in a bubble. Neither of them had been living their real life. He was based in Venice, while she lived here in London. He was a billionaire, while she was most definitely not. He owned funds and islands, private jets and helicopters and who knew what else? She owned a one-bedroom top-floor flat in Zone 3 and a six-year-old second-hand car.

What she thought she'd been doing giving him that fridge magnet she had no idea. He'd looked at it as if he'd never seen such an awful thing in his life. Clearly the sun had got to her because what on earth would a worldly billionaire with scars and an edge want with a fridge magnet? He, the man who didn't do trinkets of any kind, let alone seriously tasteless ones, was hardly going to have had a revelation about something *she'd* given him. No doubt it had gone in the bin the minute she'd left.

In fact, she'd had a lucky escape, she'd just about managed to convince herself. If things had carried on in the same vein, with that intensity, how long would it have been before she found herself so wrapped up in him she didn't want to be anywhere else? Before her identity and her independence completely disappeared? Before she became wholly reliant on him for her happiness and well-being and everything else? And see how she'd feared putting her emotions into the hands of a man? Well, she'd been right to.

She was *glad* he hadn't asked her to stay, and even gladder he'd been honest, even if it had been brutal. He'd saved her from a world of torment. Except he hadn't, because she was in torment now, and she didn't believe any of the stuff she'd been trying to tell herself anyway.

But the pain would subside eventually, she told herself wretchedly, as yet another wave of sadness washed over her, pricking her eyes and tightening her throat. She'd get over him and this endless misery. She'd got over far worse. The excruciating longing she felt when she thought about everything Georgie had would fade with time. Of course it would. She had work. She had friends. And now family. She wasn't alone.

On Monday she'd send his phone back. She had to rid herself of her ridiculous obsession with scrolling through all the photos of him she'd taken. It wasn't healthy. The amount of wine she'd consumed over the last week wasn't particularly healthy either. And as for the *linguine alla vongole* she ordered night after night from her local Italian restaurant, well, that had to stop too.

Tonight's delivery, she vowed, despondently getting to her feet in response to the buzzer and heading into the kitchen to let her favourite delivery guy in, would be the last. Because what choice did she have but to move on, however much it broke her heart?

But when she opened the door and found Rico standing there, actually there on her doorstep, holding her bag of food and looking so handsome he took her breath away, she realised she could no more move on than she could fly to the moon. She was rooted to the spot, her heart suddenly thundering and her head spinning.

'May I come in?'

His voice was gruff, and he looked as tired as she felt, and she desperately wanted to take him in her arms and smooth the exhaustion away because God, she'd missed him so much. But she didn't know why he was here, and he'd hurt her badly, so instead she lifted her chin and straightened her spine. She had to be so careful around this man.

'Sure.' She stood aside to let him in, and closed her eyes against the effect of his scent on her.

'Here,' he said, handing her the bag of food once she'd closed the door and turned back to him. 'Supper?'

'Yes,' she said, taking it from him and dumping it in the kitchen before heading onto the terrace, where at least there was air. And rosé. 'Wine?' she asked him, indicating the bottle with a wave of her hand before sitting down.

'No, thank you,' he said, folding himself into the only other chair on her balcony and fixing his gaze on her, at which point she realised that her eyes and nose were probably red and her cheeks had to be horribly blotchy, but it was too late to worry about that. He was too big for her balcony, really. Not to mention wildly out of place, with his gorgeous Italian looks and the edge that she found so attractive, while she looked a wreck. She'd been right about their lives being worlds apart. His house had a view of Venice. Hers had a view of a car park.

'So what are you doing here, Rico?' she said, unable to stand the scrutiny and the tension any longer. 'I thought you weren't planning a trip to London.'

'I went to see Finn this afternoon.'

Oh. Well. That was good. 'I'm glad.'

'It was time.'

What else might it be time for? Her? No. She was through with trying to figure out what he was thinking. 'Are you going to see him again?'

'I'm hoping to, yes.'

That was probably why he'd come. To give her an update about something he knew she cared deeply about. 'Then I guess our paths are bound to cross in the future,' she said, the smile she fixed to her face the hardest thing she'd had to do in weeks. 'But it needn't be embarrassing. You don't need to worry that I'll be making a fool of myself again. It'll be like nothing ever happened.'

He gave a harsh laugh and shoved his hands through his hair. 'Believe me, *tesoro*, that is *not* something I'm worried about.'

'Then what *are* you worried about?'

'That I might have screwed things up with you for good.'

Her heart hammered and time seemed to slow right down. 'What do you mean?'

'I'm in love with you, Carla.'

She went very still as his words hit her brain. 'What?' she breathed.

'I love you.'

'Since when?'

'Since the moment I met you, I suspect,' he

said with the faintest of smiles that faded when he added, 'I only realised it, however, two hours and thirty minutes ago. I'm sorry it took me so long to figure it out.'

'But you sent me away,' she said, desperately wanting to believe him but so very wary at the same time.

'I know.'

'You hurt me.'

'I'm so sorry. Every time I think about what I said, it kills me.'

'Why did you?'

'I've been alone a long time,' he said, holding her gaze steadily and making no attempt to dodge or deflect the question. 'It's a hard habit to break. I didn't recognise what was happening to me.' He inhaled deeply. 'The thing is, *amore mio*, when I arrived in Milan to start work, I shut myself down and put it all behind me. It was the only way I could move forward. I closed off my emotions and kept myself apart. Nothing mattered. I took risks because I had nothing to lose. I've lived like that for years. And it was fine. And then I had the accident and saw the photo of Finn and it wasn't quite so fine, although I had no idea why. You asked me why I showed up at his house. Well, I genuinely had no idea. I'd acted purely on instinct. You showed me why, Carla,' he said, leaning forwards and enveloping her with his heat and the scent she loved so much. 'And because of you I don't want to be alone any more. You were right all along. Something has been missing from my life and I know what it is now. I've been looking for a place to belong and someone to belong with ever since my parents died, and I've finally found it. With you. We *are* kindred spirits, Carla. You were right about that too. We belong together. I love you and I'm sorry beyond words that I hurt you. I asked you once before not to give up on me. And I know I don't deserve it but I'm asking you again. Please don't. I don't think I could stand losing you again.'

He stopped and looked at her, everything in his heart there for her to see in his expression. His eyes were dark and intense and the love and absolute certainty she saw in their depths shattered the fragile barrier she'd hastily erected around her heart. And suddenly she was awash with all the emotions she hadn't dared to dream.

This was what love was, she thought dizzily, revelling in the swelling of her heart and the overwhelming happiness that was now rushing through her. This. Trust and belonging and healing and the promise of forever.

'You won't,' she said, her throat tight with emotion.

'Really?'

'I never gave up on you, Rico,' she said, rising from her seat and moving towards him at the same time as he reached out and pulled her astride him, 'and I never will.' He let out a shuddering breath and dropped his head to her chest. 'I love you,' she said against his hair. 'You've shown me the life I want to live. And that life is with you. Although how we'd make it work when you live in Venice and I live in London I have no idea.'

'I can work from anywhere,' he said, lifting his head and shifting her closer. 'I have an apartment here.'

'But Venice is your home.'

'My home is wherever you are,' he said softly, taking her hand and placing it over his wildly thundering heart. 'Show me your world, Carla. It's so much brighter than mine. You've given me back hope. You've given me a future. Look.' Easing back slightly, he took his phone out of his jacket pocket and she noted that his hand was shaking a little too. After a moment he held the device up to her and she gasped. The picture was of his fridge, and there stuck right in the middle of the door, like a beacon, was her magnet.

'I assumed you'd have thrown it away,' she said, her eyes stinging as emotion overwhelmed her.

'I intended to. I couldn't. I'm done with detachment and distance,' he said gruffly. 'I want to make memories with you, *amore mio*. I want to fill our life with clutter and light and love.'

'God, I've missed you.'

'You can't have missed me as much as I've missed you,' he said with the slightest of smiles that lit up her heart. 'My life meant nothing before you crashed into it. Now it means everything. *You* mean everything. You are my *anima gemella*, my soulmate.'

'And you're mine,' she said, everything she was feeling rocketing around inside her and making her giddy. 'But it's only been a couple of weeks. It's madness.'

'We have a whole lifetime to work on the details.'

'A whole lifetime?' she echoed as he took her in his arms and pulled her as close as he could. 'I think I like the sound of that.'

'We'll figure it out together,' he said, bending his head and pressing his mouth to the sensitive spot on her neck beneath her ear and making her shiver.

'I think I like the sound of that too.'

'Il mio cuore,' he murmured, dotting a trail of kisses along her jaw.

'And that.'

And a kiss at the corner of her mouth. *'Ti amo.'*

'Especially that.'

And then he kissed her properly and carried her into her bedroom, and after that she gave up thinking at all.

EPILOGUE

Identical Strangers, 1.6 million views,
a week ago

'So APART FROM LOOKS,' came the voice of the interviewer off-screen, 'how similar are the two of you?'

'It's early days,' said Finn with an easy smile as he shifted in his seat and hooked the ankle of one leg over the knee of the other. 'But I'd say pretty similar. We're both great with numbers and mildly allergic to milk, so that's a start.'

'You're married, is that right?'

Finn gave a nod, a smile spreading across his face. 'That's absolutely right.'

'Any wedding bells on the horizon for you, Rico?' said the interviewer.

'I couldn't possibly comment,' said Rico with a smile half the size of Finn's but which lit up his face twice as much. 'All I will say is, watch this space.'

'We certainly will. Do either of you have anything else to add? Any message for your missing brother?'

'Just this,' said Rico, leaning forwards and looking seriously and directly down the lens. 'If you're out there and able to, please get in touch. Contact Alex Osborne of Osborne Investigations. We want to hear from you. And I can absolutely guarantee it'll be worth it.'

* * * * *